To Beth,
Best wishes

MATTER OVER MIND

STEVE CAPLAN | A NOVEL

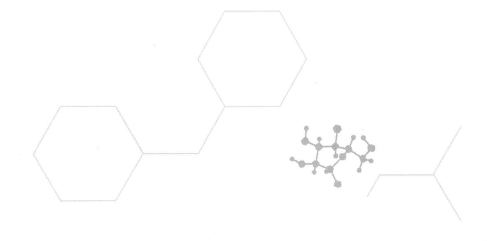

Book cover and interior design by Kim Goldberg.

ISBN: 978-0-615-39861-7

For Chubchikit — *"In sickness and in health..."*

In memory of Peggy Wheelock, Ph.D., whose tremendous contribution to basic research and outstanding dedication and commitment to the mentoring of junior researchers will be treasured forever by the next generation of scientists.

A true friend.

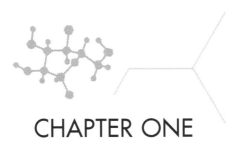

CHAPTER ONE

Never a dull moment—put three scientists in a room and get five different points of view. Ironically, I have always been certain that my friends are all convinced that biomedical research is a tedious, boring, and dull enterprise. If it is not entirely dull, then they at least expect that the people carrying it out are a quiet, reserved lot: polite and self-restrained, scientific Barney the Dinosaur characters, pipette- and flask-yielding Mr. Rogers types, or know-it-all geeks and "goody-goodies." People view us as a scientific form of chartered accountant: terribly boring and polite in their eyes, if not somewhat more honorable than the average chartered accountant. "Some of my best friends are biomedical researchers," I could imagine people saying apologetically. But there's not a chance of us sincere lackluster scientists taking part in the adventurous Enron style of "cooking the books." Fraudulent experiments simply do not hold up when the next research group tries to build on falsified data. They see us as a grounded, uninteresting form of astronaut putting his best foot forward in a valiant attempt to better humanity. Perhaps we are, but our passive and easy-going image couldn't be farther from the truth.

I took a sip of cold water from my coffee mug. I had brought the water from the cooler situated in the department hallway across from the men's room. Neal, my veteran Ph.D. student, is always on at me about the water cooler. "Steve," he says shaking his head with overdramatized awe, "how can you actually drink from that? I can see the cockroaches climbing in and out of the drain every time I go by in the hallway." I don't really know why I do drink from it; it is disgusting, and Neal is certainly telling the truth. It's sheer laziness, I suppose. The only other options are to climb up two flights of stairs to the eighth floor water cooler or to go all the way down to the cafeteria to buy a bottle of water. Neither are mind-bogglingly difficult choices, but they do take up time. And time is perhaps my most valuable asset. It is also my private nemesis. Time may not necessarily be on my side, and my dream of maintaining an independent research lab at the institute may be slipping through my fingers like sand.

Neal has just been in my comfortable little office to go over some of his recent results. The room is cozy, with a fair sized window overlooking the Toronto area. The office resembles, as Neal would say, "a fucking botanical garden." In spite of his hot-headed reactionary behavior and sharp and occasionally vulgar tongue, he has quite a talent for accumulating good results, and we have already published an article together in a relatively prestigious scientific journal. But Neal is hungry, and his ambitions are unfulfilled thus far. Basically, this is a good thing, because it leaves him extremely motivated and increases the likelihood that we might become a leading lab in our little niche. But that is still of secondary importance to me right now. I have my hands full just maintaining this job. Of course, I have my own personal stake in Neal's continued scientific accomplishments under my direction. My tenure is now a crucial issue and I need desperately to tip the balance to the publish side of the old "publish or perish" option. Professor Lewis Smithers, my clever departmental colleague and personal rival, sidled up to me just yesterday morning in the hallway with one of his typically sadistic grins fluttering on his thin lips.

"Say, Miller, did you hear about Jenkinson?"

"No," I replied with extreme caution. Smithers was dangerous. I felt almost as though I were being arrested, and I could vividly imagine the handcuffs coming out: everything you say can and will be used against you...

"He got the boot." Smithers was now smiling and rubbing his hands together with an unmasked evil glee. "The reports say that he got good recommendations from all the external reviewers. He even published two articles last year in *Journal of Biological Chemistry*. But the committee here decided that he doesn't have what it takes."

This was news to me, very bad news indeed. In fact, it truly frightened the hell out of me, but I was determined not to let Smithers see any weakness in my reaction to his information. He himself had probably sat on poor Jenkinson's internal committee and did the damage. He probably even chaired the committee, steering the members towards the sad outcome. For all I knew, he was on my own tenure committee, too. The best thing to do was to play calm, outwardly agree with Smithers, and not allow him to see me flustered. Inwardly, I was queasily shaking with mounting fear, making my own desperate calculations to assess my own chances of passing the committee.

"Oh," I answered, trying to be as flippant as possible, "I suppose the committee members know what they're doing. He probably just isn't good enough." I felt like a traitor. Bruce Jenkinson and I had practically arrived at the institute on the same day. We had each been through the myriad of complications and havoc of putting a research lab on its feet and starting from scratch. I tried not to look at Smithers' eyes.

Smithers nodded in agreement, rubbing his hands methodically as if to dry them, "Evidently not. Better to weed them out early before they take root. We don't want this institution to decline altogether."

Was Smithers treating me as a fellow colleague, an equal, someone who like himself, was naturally above such criticism?

No, I decided, Smithers would never treat me like an equal. Not even if I received tenure. I would always be below his level. Who wouldn't? After all, he was a top-notch and highly respected scientist. It was far more likely that he was trying to frighten me, to bait me, to see how much I was afraid of losing my own position. He was testing my self-confidence and digging for fear. Smithers has always had a nose for fear. I think he can smell it. And was I ever afraid! It had taken me a total of fourteen years to receive the reins of this laboratory: three years of undergraduate science, two years to receive my master's degree, another five years for my Ph.D., and finally four more years doing postdoctoral studies at the famous Wafton Institute in Boston. I imagined that poor Jenkinson had more or less "sacrificed" the same number of years to attain the goal of becoming an independent researcher. Now he was probably packing up his belongings, downloading files from his personal computer, and making SOS phone calls across the continent as he desperately searched for an opportunity elsewhere. How would he tell his wife? How would he face his students? What an awkward situation! To openly admit that the university doesn't have confidence in his abilities in front of them—how could he retain his self-esteem? Worse yet, what would his students do? He had two Ph.D. students who had started their work several years ago. They would undoubtedly need to begin anew. There was little chance of Bruce's finding another position in Toronto, not to mention anywhere else. What university would opt for an outcast, someone who had already been rejected? They were better off starting fresh with a younger, newer applicant. If our institute had "excommunicated" Bruce Jenkinson, other universities would suspect that there must be a reason. And there was, I thought grimly—people like Smithers. That wasn't entirely fair, since Smithers may not actually have been on his committee, but he certainly was in agreement with the verdict. And how could he form such an attitude without being on the committee? He must have had access to poor Jenkinson's files and information. He must have been on that committee. I resolved to call up Bruce afterwards and wish him well, although I knew he would be bitter. His family wouldn't starve, I was sure, but after dreaming of this career, running your own independent laboratory, and carrying out your own research ideas and plans, anything else was a poor substitute. If he couldn't find anything in the biotech industry, I supposed that he could always teach high school. I shuddered at the thought and tried not to think of my own, as-of-yet undetermined fate. I could always find a little lab at some unknown university in South America, perhaps in Chile or Argentina, and make my own little kingdom even if the money for research was poor. Anything would be better than humiliating myself teaching high school. I might not stay at the forefront of research, but at least I would fight to stay in the minor leagues if necessary. But now I still had a shot at the major leagues, and I wasn't prepared to let Smithers push me around. At least not yet.

Although my own position was extremely unstable, it was still not a lost cause. Neal's success "at the bench," his series of experimental findings, was proving fruitful for me. Every new piece of data that he uncovers, every slice of new information that he derives working with me, every discovery, and every successful experiment will ultimately lead to peer-reviewed scientific publications and the "Holy Grail"—grant money. These are the very things that I desperately need to enhance my job security. And my job will not be secure until the committee had assured me of tenure. Until then I am as dispensable as a plastic test tube—or a 7-Eleven drinking cup—just like poor Jenkinson. Neal is well aware of my situation, and he has been a bulldozer in clearing the way towards the "mission impossible" called tenure. Although Neal's loyalty to me is beyond question, he certainly has his own stakes in not seeing me pack my suitcases and leave the department. He would not relish the prospect of finding another supervisor in the middle of his Ph.D. research; starting all over from scratch would be daunting. Additionally, finding another advisor who would put up with his rather blunt behavior might be another serious issue. Neal also knows that his loyalty is a long-term investment. One day, in a number of years, he might be standing in my very position. Even as a student he has the foresight to understand that in future years, researchers such as myself—assuming that I do not get tossed out of the system—might help determine his own fate. But now I was way ahead of myself, daydreaming again. I must not take anything for granted.

Not all my colleagues, however, share my grave doubts about my chances of becoming a tenured faculty member. Professor Davis, that old gambler, has even been trying to get me to wager with him. But I cannot bring myself to bet against my own tenure; it's a conflict of interest. Aside from that, I am not willing to give up my new fluorescent microscope to Arthur. He just doesn't deserve it. He hasn't brought in a dime of grant money to the department for years. In fact, for some time, I have felt that Arthur Davis is acutely jealous of my newly developing lab. My mainstream interests are becoming ever more popular in the scientific community, and this is of prime importance in obtaining grant money for research. My specialties lie particularly in the biological and molecular mechanisms involved in mental disorders, especially depression. It seems that all the students attracted to work for me thus far, including the postdoc/technician called Singh, have their own vested interests in understanding the mechanisms of depressive disorders. Neal once confided in me that his mother had been severely depressed throughout his childhood. Neal himself also has a mild form of dyslexia, and he frequently comes to work wearing his favorite "I Dyslexia Love" T-shirt. Singh's brother is a schizophrenic. Tania, my new Ph.D. student, professed to me that her uncle had psychotic depressive tendencies. My new master's student, Ken, has not yet mentioned any family connection with depression, but I am willing to bet that with time one will be uncovered. Ken has only been with us a few months and he's not very talkative; he probably feels that he's got to get over the student stage and complete his academic courses successfully before he feels more at home in the lab and with Neal, Tania, Singh, and me. However, looking at the pattern, including my own reasons for choosing such a line of research, I doubt that Ken is here by any coincidence.

I think back a few minutes to my meeting with Neal. He always starts these conversations with his obligatory and somewhat obsessive complaints. "Jesus, Steve, is this a second class research joint or what? Don't tell me it's like this in the States, too."

"What's the problem this time, Neal?"

"I got here this morning a little late, after Opera-Singh had already started, but he was practically working in the dark," Neal ranted.

"Opera-Singh" was the name that we had unanimously coined for Singh; he was crazy about operas and Neal often complained that he would awaken at night in a cold sweat, suffering from palpitations and the noise of heavy nasal voices humming *Carmen*. That was before I decided to split my forces and keep the two of them in the adjacent but separate labs. I am still debating whether to move Ken in with Opera-Singh or with Neal and Tania. Not that Tania is a problem to get along with.

"So?" I queried. "You know that he often works in the dark. Let him. Why should you care, you've got your own lab to work in?" This was true; my little kingdom here at the University Center for Disease Research was composed of two separate but joined laboratories and my little office just down the hallway.

"But the reason," Neal blurted out, "it's so bloody stupid that it hurts—it's not even Opera-Singh's fault this time." Coming from Neal, this was a major concession.

"Well," I replied, "are you going to keep me in suspense for much longer? I'd really like to get some work done today. You know that we both could be out on the streets looking for work in the next few weeks."

Neal sat before me, smirking slightly. We had a tacit understanding about my tenure situation, with each of us referring to it only indirectly.

"Is he on at you again?" he said, hooking his thumb in the direction of Smithers' office.

"Never mind," I countered, trying to be offhanded. "Just get to the point."

Neal's veins were almost popping out of his forehead. His closely cropped hair showed signs of receding like a glacier during global warming. This only enhanced the danger signals evident in his pulsating blood vessels. To some extent, he reminded me of myself, ten years earlier. I, too, had once been even more obsessive and a rather excitable character; I was highly motivated and extremely volatile. But since receiving my position as an independent investigator, something in me had relaxed. Perhaps it was an anticlimax, after so many years of dreaming and striving to prove myself worthy. Maybe it was simply resignation. This Canadian institution would never be on par with the top American institutes where I did my postdoctoral work, no matter what the University President proclaimed in his weekly propaganda releases to the local press: "Cancer cured again and again by institute investigators." Well why were people still dying of cancer? In any case, Neal did not yet know that our institute would never be top tier, or at least he didn't believe it. And I did not want to damage his motivation at this stage. Let him see for himself in a few years' time.

Neal breathed deeply, "Get this. Three out of the nine neon lights in Opera-Singh's lab have burned out. He claims that he called maintenance to come and replace them, but they—"

I cut him off. "But they say 'after the Christmas holidays.'" It was only mid-November, of course.

"No!" Neal ejaculated, all revved up now like a turbo engine, "They say that due to budget constraints each lab will only have two-thirds of their fluorescent lights working. Only if another light burns out in Opera-Singh's lab will they come and replace it. And only that particular one!"

Neal was now livid with anger, trembling like a leaf in a in a sudden gust of wind. Even I was surprised at the level that this university could sink to. A bottomless pit, apparently. Next thing you know, they'll be charging me for the electricity and water that I use in the lab, too.

I picked up my phone and dialed Hugo's number. Hugo was the department "do-all." What he really did, though, was absolutely nothing. Usually we preferred when he was doing nothing, because when he was actually doing something, it was inevitably related to the recruitment of students, lecturers, or generally unlucky passers-by to his reborn-Christian meetings. Neal practically shrank from Hugo, presenting with symptoms resembling a panic attack. Somewhat surprisingly, having Hugo around was actually good for the atmosphere in my lab; he allowed a union of forces, albeit temporarily, between Neal and Opera-Singh, both of whose opinions of Hugo wavered between disdain and utter disgust.

"Hugo," I said into the phone, "would you please stop by for a minute."

"Hallelujah, Steve, God willing I'll be right there." I could already see Neal cringe at hearing the twang of Hugo's nasal voice.

Neal scratched his left ear and stared at me with a look of pure skepticism. "You don't really think Hugo is going to be of any help, do you?"

"Of course not," I said cynically, imitating Neal's tone of irritation, "but let's not get him angry at us for going over his head."

"If we did to him what King Henry the Eighth did to two of his wives, we wouldn't *have* to go over it anymore," he muttered sullenly.

Hugo arrived and sat down in my office in the empty chair beside Neal. He was a thin man of medium height with narrow shoulders and small brown eyes. He wore a rather sparse moustache proclaiming his masculinity via testosterone-induced facial hair. He came to work every day with his battered attaché case, wearing scuffed and peeling dress shoes, wrinkled dress pants, and a button-down shirt that never properly concealed his white tank top. He also made a habit of really overdoing the aftershave. Neal would often complain, "He's barely got whiskers, why does he have to shave every day? He smells like a fucking perfume department. When he gets near the lab, before I even realize it's him, I foam at the mouth afraid that the organic chemists downstairs are terrorizing us again with their bloody concoctions." Opera-Singh, whose sense of smell had never been very good, had different ideas. "If de department vuh able to dispense of Mr. Gunther, shuhly ve could find bettah vays to utilize the money saved." No doubt Opera-Singh had plans of his own to set up a speaker system so that he could listen to his operas from any of the labs in the department.

"How's everything, Hugo?" I ventured politely as Hugo sidled into my office.

"Praise be the lord, wonderful. No problem at all," Hugo answered automatically. I could see Neal pivot in his seat and glance at his watch. I noticed that his nostrils were quivering slightly, perhaps in a vain attempt to avoid breathing in Hugo's all-embracing aftershave.

"Listen, Hugo. The good lord once said 'Let there be light,' isn't that so?"

"Hallelujah, Hallelujah. Thus sayeth the Lord, and light there was," replied Hugo.

"Well listen, then, Hugo. The maintenance department here at the university has a bone to pick with God. Three out of the nine fluorescent bulbs in Opera-Singh's lab are out, and the chaps at maintenance refuse to obey the good lord and provide us with light. We could really use the light, you know—it's surprisingly helpful with the research."

"Sorry, Steve, those are orders from the top. The university has decided that this way they can cut down on one-third of the electricity resulting from lighting the buildings."

Neal was about to say something, perhaps a sarcastic comment about the possibility of ordering night vision goggles, but I cut him off abruptly preempting him with a wave of my hand. "Listen, Hugo, we need the light. What happens if I order three more desktop fluorescent lights for each lab. Will that mean that the university will have to give us three more working neons?"

Hugo thought for a moment. Neal later would claim that he could hear the wheels clicking in his head, the isolated IQ beads knocking into each other as the process of thought perforated through his brain. Indeed, Neal would often groan that Hugo's problems could be resolved rather easily by a simple IQ transplant. "Yes sirree, praise the lord, that's true. But you'll have to pay for the new light fixtures through your own research budget."

"Fine," I agreed, "just do it quickly please, before we need to bring light bulbs from home in order to work, or even candles." I recalled a story Neal had told me some time ago. While working at the department where he had obtained his master's degree, there had been a month when Neal received his monthly scholarship receipt with seventy-five dollars deducted for electricity. Neal claimed that he had gone directly to his lab supervisor, who was also his employer, and said, "Professor Winters, I know that I may have forgotten to turn off the lights one evening when closing up the lab, but isn't that a little too steep?" It had eventually turned out that a guest professor whose name was also Neal Parsons had been staying at a university guest residence, and that somehow there had been a real mix-up. Neal lamented, "These mix-ups are never in my favor somehow." It's hard to disagree with that.

Once Hugo was gone, Neal furtively asked me whether he should raid Jenkinson's lab and grab all the fluorescents and light bulbs before they disappeared anyway. I could see that he was well informed and had already heard of Jenkinson's sad fate. But I wouldn't allow him to land on poor Bruce's lab like an eagle in for the kill. It was too vulgar. I eventually shunted Neal back off to work, with a few new ideas to play with, some articles to dig up in order to see whether they contained methods applicable to our research, and lots of new experiments to plan. Neal was the type that always had to be busy, he always had to have ten things cooking at the same time. Of course he complained about the masses of work and pressure that I constantly put him through, but he enjoyed the work. "Happy like a pig in shit," he himself would say. And I usually managed to supply him with his necessary "shit."

I sat down and tried to get myself organized. The key for me was to set up weekly lists and schedules of important things to do and keep crossing them off in real time as I managed to accomplish them. Unfortunately, crises with university bureaucracy, Neal, and Opera-Singh were not included in my lists of accomplishments. These were daily issues that had to be defused as they came along. No wonder so few of us actually received tenure and were kept on at the university. Between the bureaucracy and squabbling within the lab, I felt better prepared to be a kindergarten teacher. Maybe Jenkinson couldn't handle that part of the work. I knew him from way back and was sure that he was qualified to do first class research. Perhaps he didn't have the management skills. But as these thoughts flooded my brain, I remembered Smithers' sadistic grin and decided that this was unlikely. Oh shit! I had to stop this. I wouldn't be able to get anything done if I kept thinking of the future. I had to go step by step. I looked at my list for this week. My main occupation should be gathering ideas for a new proposed grant application. This application was focused on studying a horrifying, debilitating mental illness known as "manic-depressive disorder." It has more recently become known as "bipolar disorder," due to its habit of swinging the patient's mental status back and forth from severe depression to manic highs. Although I had built up my reputation and the lab on the more common depressive and anxiety disorders, I think that ultimately I had always intended to diverge into studies of this illness. Unlike the other depressive disorders, of which many could be induced chemically in animals, this particular illness is especially difficult to study since no animal model is available. For this reason, this type of research requires a very close collaboration between basic researchers, such as myself, and qualified psychiatrists. Fortunately, a new psychiatrist here at the adjacent hospital, Dr. Julia Kearns, is very interested in a collaborative effort. I have promised Julia that I will have an outline ready for her to read and critique by the end of the week. However, each time I finally manage to sit down and disentangle myself from Neal, Opera-Singh, and the others, I just can't seem to concentrate on the proposal. I sit here facing my computer and feel its hypnotic effect sweeping me back years and years to my childhood in that cold, snowy prairie city of Regina.

• • • • • • • • •

One of my earliest childhood memories was a feeling of sharp, bipolar contrast. I'm not altogether sure I understand exactly what induced that predominant feeling. Perhaps it was a plethora of emotions that added up to forge a feeling of contrast, or conflict if you will. My first memories and images of the noble figure of Grandpa Joe must have been formed when I was no older than three or four years of age. He was pulling his heavy brown woolen sweater tightly about him, opening both the massive wooden front door and the transparent screen door to pop outside into the freezing Regina air and extract the mail from our mailbox. Despite the shining sun and clear blue skies, I can still remember the icicles hanging from the roof gutters like stalactites in a limestone cave. Grandpa Joe would shiver abruptly, quickly closing the doors and hopping back into our well heated house on Wascana Drive.

Grandpa Joe would notice me watching him and would speak to me, his oldest grandson, in his gruff Russian-accented bass voice. Despite living in Canada since he was twelve years old, one of his deepest regrets was that he would never master the Canadian accent; thus, he would always feel himself a foreigner. If there was one thing that Grandpa Joe wished for himself, it was to get rid of that heavy foreign accent, especially since it was Russian. Grandpa Joe hated the communists and anything associated with socialism. This he would tell us over and over. Even the color red would infuriate him. The sight of a red shirt or dress could easily provoke Grandpa Joe into acting like a bull in a china shop. Whenever he drove us anywhere in his blue Pontiac, we would inevitably hear his symbolic interpretation of intersection lights. "That's exactly vot the communists vant to do," he would explain, "to stop everything vith their red orientation." He would always be the only one in our family to voice his support for Nixon and later Reagan. When I reached high school he tried desperately to indoctrinate me with Ayn Rand's *Atlas Shrugged*, though I had already got the gist of it from *The Fountainhead*. Although he was not a hockey fan, the 1980 nonprofessional U.S. Olympic Hockey Team's "Miracle on Ice" win over the Soviet Union served as inspiration to him throughout his life.

Grandpa Joe's Russian accent continually symbolized for him an inability to completely escape from communist Russia, even though his parents had brought him here so many years ago. Later in my life I learned that the ability to conquer new accents and intonations of speech is directly related to musical ability. Those blessed with a musical ear are best able to imitate and learn new accents. To me this seems very logical; I can remember many a time when Grandpa Joe would begin humming or singing along with songs on the radio. When this happened, my brother Ervin, my sister Cindy, and I would all whisk ourselves out of the room, like rats out of an aqueduct.

"Vere you going?" Grandpa Joe would ask innocently.

"Uh, I've got some homework to do, Grandpa," I would reply.

Little Cindy would answer, "I wanna play with my dolls."

Ervin, the most brazen of the three of us, would be more likely to say, "Got to get my earplugs fixed, grandpa."

However, nothing would ever faze Grandpa Joe. He was too good natured and loved his grandchildren too much. Grandpa Joe was there for us whenever we needed him for most of our childhood. He served a triple role—as father, mother, and grandfather. Our father was a very sick man. He became ill with that terrible disease known as manic-depressive bipolar disorder early in my childhood. Grandpa Joe, who is still caring tenderly for his only son today, recently told me that he thinks Grandma Sara's tragic death may have been the trigger for dad's illness.

"After the car accident, your father vas very depressed. It was extremely difficult for me, but your father pretty much collapsed after the accident. Since then, he has never been the same."

My earliest memories of dad are of him stationed in his room for days at a time. Although this was really both my parents' room, Ervin, Cindy, and I always referred to it as "dad's room," because he spent so much more time there than mom did. Grandpa Joe would bring dad trays of his own home cooked food, most of which would be returned uneaten to the kitchen. I don't really know what dad ate during those prolonged periods, excepting wads of pills of all colors. There were red ones, green ones, yellow ones, and blue ones, round ones, elliptical ones, square ones, and rectangular ones. Ervin used to joke that we could use them for hotels in Monopoly. At any rate, Grandpa Joe did so much more than take care of dad; he took care of us all, including mom. He bought groceries, cooked, cleaned, and did laundry. He drove us to school in his car in the winter when it was too cold to walk and prepared our lunches for us when we were still too young to do that for ourselves.

Ervin was forever complaining, "I hate tuna fish, why does he keep giving me tuna sandwiches? I can't even trade them with anyone at school because they're so disgusting. And they always get squished too." But for all his complaints, Ervin would never voice them directly to Grandpa Joe. At that age, I wasn't much help either. I would sidle up to Grandpa Joe, proudly busy in the kitchen with his 'I'm the chef' apron tied on, and say to him: "Ervin really loves those tuna sandwiches. It's amazing, I prefer the turkey breast, but he just won't try anything new."

"Don't you worry," Grandpa Joe would say to me, charged with his prophetic wisdom, "he'll grow out of it. One day he'll ask to try a different sandwich. But until then, I'm happy to make him his favorite tuna sandwich every day."

To Ervin, I'd say as we walked to school in the morning on the days when weather permitted, "Just don't disappoint Grandpa Joe, you know how hard he tries for us." When I think back on these troubled times and my petty meanness, I feel that I am wasted in my scientific career; I should have become a lawyer or gone into politics. On the other hand, I realized sadly, with fellow colleagues like Smithers, and with Bruce getting the axe, there's certainly no lack of politics in my chosen vocation.

Ultimately, the most difficult set of contrasts that I was forced to endure throughout my childhood was entirely unrelated to the weather; neither the frigid Saskatchewan winters nor the comfortably heated house caused any major problem. The most difficult thing to swallow, without a doubt, was dad's erratic behavior. My childhood memories of dad are split into two distinct phases, with short but relief filled gaps between them. The first phase, and the more dominant one, at least time-wise, was dad's depressive phase. Dad would retreat to his bedroom, preferring solitary confinement and camping out in there for days and even weeks at a time. There was no way to reach him. We children had to be extremely careful not to antagonize dad or make excessive noise. "Is this too loud?" Ervin would probe the situation with his toy trumpet.

"Ervin, go outside please, if you vant to use that thing," Grandpa Joe would beg.

"But the Taylors next door threatened to call the police last time I played the trumpet outside," Ervin would argue.

"But Ervin," I reminded him, "you were practicing at four in the morning."

"It's a good thing ve didn't get him a set of drums," Grandpa Joe would mutter.

It was never clear to any of us what would cause dad to retreat to his room and ignore us for so long. One time I can remember coming home from school when I must have been seven or eight years of age. Even before leaving the school premises, I had needed the toilet but opted to wait it out and use the cleaner and more comfortable facilities at home. When I opened the front door I had only one thing on my mind—to relieve myself as fast as possible. I made a dash straight for the toilet, unable to contain myself even a few seconds longer. Dad was so insulted that I didn't first come into the kitchen to greet him that he retreated immediately to his bedroom, slamming the door violently behind him. I tried to explain to him that I had needed the toilet badly, but dad was already unavailable, withdrawn for another few weeks into his own lonely and depressed world. When mom came home from work at the hospital that evening, I explained to her what happened.

Mom, unlike dad, had her feet firmly on the ground. She understood exactly what was going on. She was just so busy between her private ear, nose, and throat practice and her operations at the hospital that she had very limited time to spend with us. For this reason, Grandpa Joe served as our real mother too. Years later, I would realize that mom spent much more time at the hospital than necessary; it was her way of keeping her sanity. As much as she wanted to be with us kids and did, in her own way, try to shield us from dad's wrath and despair, she needed some distance from our home to keep herself "normal." Without this method of maintaining her normality, she would claim years later in talks with me, she wouldn't have been able to help us at all. The situation would have sucked her in like the undertow. I think that I understand this now, but I certainly didn't back then.

When I tried to explain to mom what had happened with dad, I broke down and began to cry. "It's all right," she would say. "I'm here now, and so is Grandpa Joe. Things will get better. It takes time." She would try to explain the situation to me with her cool, rational perspective: "You must understand, Steve, that dad has an illness. He loves you all, and wants to get better. It's not his fault that he's feeling rotten, it's an illness. It's like when you catch a cold or have an upset stomach. You can't help how you feel."

I would strive to understand, but although I had begun to read early and even skipped a grade in school, fundamental psychiatry was still several years beyond my reach. "But when I get sick, I don't blame anyone. I like when Grandpa helps by bringing me chicken soup, and when Ervin helps by not doing imitations of people vomiting. Why can't dad see that we want to help?"

Mom would try to be patient and explain, but psychology, especially child psychology, was definitely not her specialty. "Your dad's illness is something in his mind, something that makes him feel very bad, and he can't help feeling that way. Eventually, he'll get better, and then your dad will be himself again."

However, my most vivid memories of dad "as himself" were those of him barricaded in his room, with all of us tiptoeing cautiously around the house.

There were some good periods, too. With or without the influence of various antidepressants, dad would eventually crawl out of his shell and respond to his surroundings. These were great times for us all, especially Grandpa Joe. During these stints, Grandpa Joe would spend more time at the office of his wholesale clothing factory, where he had created an administrative position for dad when he was well enough to work. Dad had degrees in economics and in business administration, but I doubt that any degree or qualifications could compete with Grandpa Joe's uncanny business sense. Grandpa Joe could do no wrong in his business endeavors. He had built up the factory from scratch. We children did not learn of Grandpa Joe's capabilities from his own accounts; he was far too modest for that. Our knowledge came from mom, other members of the family, and even dad, in his rare communicative interludes. During these remissions, dad would surface and gather himself together, showing up at his office at work, smartly dressed and shaved, with his trim attaché case by his side. Looking at dad, one could never have guessed that he spent perhaps half his life (or so it seemed) hiding out behind his bedroom door. Grandpa Joe was ecstatic during these times. Although he should have known, as a grown-up, that dad's illness would not shrivel and disappear, the illusion and hope were all too much for him. He would beam with pride and tell us how the factory would grow and develop now, with dad to lead the expansion. We would cheer and really believe that things would be different. As children, it was easy to believe this. We wanted a normal father, a father who would work and come home and spend time with us. We even argued less amongst ourselves—at least for the first three or four times. By the fourth or fifth time that dad pulled himself out of one of his depressive phases, Ervin and I had already started to become skeptical. Ervin would say to me, "Place your bet, Stevie, when will dad stop going to work and stay in bed again all day? Two to one it's before the end of the week."

Grandpa Joe, overhearing these conversations would quietly intervene, "Ervin, Steve, stop it. That's your father you're talking about. He's getting better. Let's stay optimistic." Grandpa Joe never lost his optimism regarding his only son. Or so we felt all those years.

Even today, as a rational adult, and moreover, as a scientist who studies the molecular aspects of depressive disorders, I still find it difficult to recall the "real dad." We knew that side of him ever so briefly, in those golden periods when he was "himself," as Grandpa Joe used to say. The images of dad's more difficult phases are so strong, for my brother, sister, and me, that none of us were really sure who or what our real dad was. It may just be an illusion Grandpa Joe dreamed up to keep us hoping along with him. I do not know. Hopefully, grim looking vengeful characters like Smithers will not prevent me from trying to elucidate the scientific mysteries of this horrific illness that has played havoc with my family for so many years.

CHAPTER TWO

The phone rang violently and abruptly knocked me out of my reverie. I felt like a pilot who had just been ejected from his cockpit after a tense dogfight. I hate that bloody phone, but this time I was glad that it gave me a chance to stop daydreaming and begin planning my grant application. Grant funding is crucial to our research. Without it, no ideas can be tested, no matter how original and exciting. In the long run, grant money provides a direct path to tenure. The more money in my budget, the more students and equipment I can muster for experiments. This means faster results and more publications. But my allotted time for proving myself is beginning to run thin. Receiving grant funding also has a more immediate impact on my job security. Most grants are competitive and peer reviewed, so a successful grant application provides additional evidence of my research capabilities. More importantly, the institute thrives on its researchers' grant funding and would always find a way to skim off a nice chunky percentage of the money for "overhead costs."

I let the phone ring several times to give me a few seconds to compose myself and then answered in my gruff businesslike voice. The artificial gruffness was a useful ploy that I had picked up, finding that it tended to seriously limit the number of people who would call and waste my time.

"How's it going, Steve?" I could hear the calm voice of Dr. Julia Kearns, the psychiatrist here at the hospital who had agreed to collaborate with me on this as-of-yet unwritten grant application that seems to render me in a perpetual mode of procrastination.

I could feel my pulse beating rapidly in my throat as I answered as calmly, I hoped, as Julia sounded to me. I also tried to let the gruffness dissipate gradually, as though a hoarse throat had been ailing me all morning. "Not too badly, Julia. How are things at the hospital?" I felt somewhat silly asking, as though we were speaking long distance; the hospital was only next door, connected to our institute by an elaborate labyrinth of underground tunnels. I used to joke that the architects who designed the place were really psychologists in disguise. Bored with their studies of rats in mazes, they had expanded their experiments to see how scientists managed to navigate through their gigantic mazes. Neal took my jokes seriously and actually believed that there were university psychologists observing us and watching how we coped under stressful conditions, like those when the university cut off the air conditioners in mid-August last summer. Sometimes I'm inclined to believe Neal and empathize with his dose of paranoia.

"Are you free for lunch, Steve?" asked Julia, in that patient, tactful manner of hers.

"I'd love to, Julia, but I'm not making as much progress as I'd like on this grant application."

"Come on, Steve, you've got to eat anyway. Half an hour won't make or break your day, will it?"

"You're right, Julia. I'll meet you in the cafeteria. Can you give me a few minutes to check up on the lab? I haven't been in there all morning and better make sure that Neal and Opera-Singh haven't started a nuclear war in there."

"Alright, Steve, but ten minutes is ten minutes. I'm hungry."

I put down the phone and unlocked my desk drawer to get

my wallet out. It's amazing the number of thefts that occur in a scientific research department that's supposed to have restricted access by the general public. Despite beefed up security to stave off the animal rights activists, last week someone even managed to pilfer Professor Smithers' wallet from his office desk. I don't envy the culprit if Smithers ever lays his tentacles on him. I wandered over to my two lab rooms. Tania's tall, lean body was bent over an ice bucket on her bench, and she was carefully extracting the liquid supernatant from an array of tiny tubes professionally known as "Eppendorfs". I said hello but elected not to bother her. Although Tania had been with us for several months, she was still learning the tricks of the trade and wasn't yet able to do more than one thing at a time. If she was engaged in any kind of experiment when the phone rang, she would let it ring if no one else was around to answer. In addition, my presence undoubtedly made her nervous. I considered Tania to be a good student with much potential. It might take her some time to get into the full swing of things, but Neal, among his assets, was a very good teacher and full of energy. Tania, in my view, might never be as quick as Neal, but she would certainly be capable of carrying out fine work, especially if I were to continue to monitor her progress. I slid out into the other lab, only to find Opera-Singh on the rave. "Steve, I cannot do the necessary experiments prescribed without the necessary apparatus to do the work," cried out Opera-Singh in his pronounced East Indian accent, obviously in distress.

"What apparatus is it that you need?" I questioned trying to calm him down.

"It is of utmost significance that the plastic container with the thermostat and heater be returned to me immediately." He meant the water bath. We had several plastic water baths in the lab that were used to heat up water for various reactions.

Without really having to know the answer, I asked, "Where's the water bath? We have three of them anyway."

His answer did not come to me as a surprise. "Mr. Neal took my water bath. He put it in the cold room. Why put a water bath in the cold room? I am needing it here in the lab."

I knew the answer to that, too. After all, it had been my idea. Neal often needed to carry out reactions at sixteen degrees Celsius. By filling the bath and putting it in the four degrees cold room, he could get the thermostat to heat the bath to exactly sixteen degrees. Otherwise the water in the bath would simply rise to room temperature, which was about twenty-two degrees, at least today.

I said to Opera-Singh, "But Singh (we never called him Opera-Singh to his face), you have two other water baths, what's wrong with them?"

"They are being too big for me," he said with an expansive gesture of his arms. "It is being very bad for bath and thermostat to be in cold room—it cause malfunction."

One thing about Opera-Singh that could drive me out of my mind was his empathy for machines. He was an absolute expert on what was good and what was bad for every machine, electronic device, or apparatus. Neal would often claim that Opera-Singh had been a bench-top centrifuge, electrical power supply, and a wealth of other lab gadgets in previous reincarnations. "How else could he know what's 'good' and what's 'bad' for these things? It doesn't even say what's good or bad for them in the fucking instruction manuals."

I breathed deeply, counted to three silently, and then patiently explained, "Look, Singh, I realize that it's more difficult for you to use the larger water baths, but there's not a lot of room for the larger ones in the cold room. That's probably why Neal took the one you prefer." I was careful not to say "yours" to Singh, because that would give him charge over the stupid water bath and Neal would come rushing at me to complain.

"That's exactly why I took the small bath," called out the culprit from over my shoulder, as he charged headlong into the lab.

"Look fellows, maybe you're old enough to sort this out for yourselves, okay. I'm going down for a bite to eat in the cafeteria and should be back in a half hour or so if you need me."

Neal looked at me in astonishment. "When did you get your hepatitis A shot? Are you sure you're feeling okay? A friend of mine tried the food there last week and—"

I cut him off, "Come on Neal, you'll kill my appetite. Don't forget I've been through Bolivia, Peru, and Ecuador and managed to survive. Give me a break."

• • • • • • • • •

"So how's Debby adjusting to first grade?" I asked Julia as we sat in an isolated corner of the cafeteria with our trays of food. I glanced down at the plate of yellowish rice and tried to forget Neal's comments about the food. I looked up at Julia; she was an attractive woman of about thirty-five years of age. She had light brown hair that fell in waves to her rounded shoulders and bright hazel eyes. When she smiled, I could see a flash of her straight white teeth. Her clothes were quite modest; in fact they were more fitting for researchers—designed more for comfort than for fashion. In my view, Julia did not need any additional help to expose or emphasize her own natural beauty; she was simply stunning, in a very wholesome sort of way. However, despite my attraction to her, physically and otherwise, I was striving to keep myself at a professional distance. After a string of unsuccessful relationships, culminating in a short marriage and divorce, I did not feel ready to spoil another one. And this particular theoretical one seemed to possess special meaning for me. I was convinced that the time was not yet ripe; Julia and I would remain collaborators at work and avoid mixing business and pleasure. I just hoped that by the time I finally sorted myself out, if and when I ever received my tenure at the institute, Julia would still be available. After all, beautiful, intelligent divorcees are always in demand. She may want more children, I reasoned, and she's soon approaching that age where things can be complicated.

"Debby's doing fine," she answered simply. While quizzing Julia about her daughter, I wondered whether she had any inkling about my rapidly developing feelings towards her. I hadn't consciously done much to give myself away. No, I guessed that she was still unaware of my attraction to her. After all, I convinced myself, she's only a psychiatrist, not a bloody mind reader.

"Great," I encouraged her, "but then I suppose you know how to prepare a child for such adjustments."

Julia laughed, but looked at me seriously. "How are you adjusting at work?"

"Well, I suppose that dealing with characters like Neal and Opera-Singh (Julia was not only familiar with the names of my co-workers, but had also seen them in action several times upon visiting the lab), I too could use a psychiatrist."

Julia laughed again, throwing back her pretty face. She knew just what I meant. "How's the grant application coming along?"

I must have cringed slightly, because Julia said, "Did I say something wrong?"

"No, no of course not. I just feel badly that I haven't even finished the first draft yet, and I know that I promised to let you read it by this week."

"Steve, that's alright. I know that you have your hands full. It doesn't matter that much to me. It would be nice if we could get our hands on that money, but regardless I think that our plan to collaborate is a good idea, and even if we don't get the money for that project, there's still room to maneuver. I know for a fact that there is almost no good research that combines clinical and basic studies the way we'd like to. I can get you all the blood samples from my patients, categorized properly according to the degree of the illness. This could open all kinds of new windows for us both."

Was she hinting at more than just research? I didn't know. It was not easy to interpret Julia's thoughts; she kept her cards pretty close to her chest.

We finished our "gourmet lunch," as Neal would refer to it, and parted. I promised to have the draft ready for her inspection within a few days, and she promised to keep in touch.

The elevators in our institute were on strike again and I

climbed up the six flights of stairs gingerly. I wondered how old Professor Winston could possibly get up to the fifth floor where he worked when the elevators were out. I supposed that he would sit in the library on the main floor and wait for the servicemen to fix the elevators. I tried to remember to ask Neal about that. He always knew the answers to these types of institutional trivia.

When I finally got back to my department, I decided to first head back to my office and compose myself before walking into the lab. I was completely exhausted by the six flights of stairs, and I didn't feel like hearing Neal's wisecracks. I sat down in my chair to catch my breath and pushed the button on my answering machine to play back the messages. Nothing especially interesting was awaiting my attentions on the machine. There was a message from Jeannie, my ex-wife from years gone by. I knew what she wanted, but I wasn't particularly keen to give it to her. Since our separation five years ago, we had been co-guardians of our now eight-year-old dog Compo. Compo was a mongrel; I envisioned that he was a cross between a cocker spaniel and a donkey based on his size, appearance, and temperament. We had picked up Compo from a very musical family when he was a small puppy only three months old. The father was actually a composer—hence the name Compo, which stuck with us too. We had originally taken on Compo as a sort of mini-trial, to see whether we were worthy of being parents, even to a dog. Whether we were worthy parents or not, one can only ask Compo. However, as a couple, we did not last very long; our marriage fizzled out rather quickly, and Compo was sentenced to a life of dual custody, rotating between the two of us every few months or so. Truthfully, I think that over the past two years Compo has been spending more and more time at my flat. As intelligent and loving as he is to have around, he does present certain problems. First of all, with Compo at home, I must get out of the lab early enough to let him out in the evenings or else come back to the lab later to finish my work. Another problem with Compo is his "Bafu," the Portugese word (that I learned from a Brazilian friend of mine) for halitosis.

Compo's breath could make cheese curdle. It could probably make meat, rocks, mountains, and glaciers curdle as well. Even my dirty socks would lean in the other direction when they saw Compo's tongue hanging out. Repeated attempts to address this issue at the veterinarian's office led me to purchase a toothbrush for him and have his gums cleaned. Brushing his teeth turned out to be a joke that only exposed me to blasts of his breath from close range. Having his gums cleaned did little to offset the smell. I basically gave up, deciding that he would never have sweet-smelling breath, and that my best strategy was to distance myself from his mouth, especially when he was panting. However, Compo's most serious drawback is a psychological one. Perhaps it's the classical abandoned child syndrome, the same feeling a child gets when his parents separate and live apart. Compo has become unbalanced in this sense. The mere sight of a suitcase or backpack is enough to draw him into deep depression. If I hadn't liked dogs so much, Compo in particular, I might have toyed with the idea of inducing canine depression as a model for our studies in the lab. However, any work with dogs was absolutely out of the question. Once depressed, Compo was not willing to suffer anyone's affections, except my own or Jeannie's. In other words, Compo would not hesitate to bite anyone who dared linger a hand within a specific radius of his mouth.

At any rate, I was in no hurry to return Jeannie's call and preferred to keep Compo with me as long as possible, despite the responsibility and added burden.

I listened to the other messages. There was also a call from Jim, who apparently wanted to try to get me to come out for dinner together with him, his wife Carol, and a date for me. I was very leery of these attempted setups, but there came a point when I couldn't refuse all the time. I called Jim back at his office, put up a valiant fight, and finally agreed to go out somewhere with them and have dinner afterwards.

"Any preference where you'd like to go?" Jim asked politely.

"No," I answered. "No, wait, hang on—just not the opera! If I hear *Carmen* again I think I might strangle someone."

"Okay, take it easy, don't worry," Jim reassured me. He was also aware of the effects of Opera-Singh and Neal on my affections for various forms of culture.

I began to collect my thoughts again, with the hope of finally focusing them on my grant application. Before I could even turn on my computer, the telephone rang again. With practiced indifference I reached over to the wall plug and plucked the connection out of the wall. This little action did wonders and the phone stopped ringing instantly. I then got up and closed the door to my office, pulling the little shade down so that any potential time-consuming intruders lurking outside wouldn't find sanctuary in here with me. I leafed through stacks of research papers, references to be quoted in my proposal, and began my task in earnest. The outline gradually began to take shape and I even formed a few ideas on how to attack the specific aims. When I am left alone to my own devices, I can concentrate and even work quickly. The problem, as always, is those unplanned interruptions that are so common. I was making good progress and starting to think of calling it a day when I heard a knock on my door.

"Yes, Neal?" Neal had a very distinctive knock.

"Your phone is out of order," he said. "You better let them know, or you won't have any telecommunications until after Christmas."

"You mean after New Year's, Neal. I'm surprised at you. No one will fix anything between Christmas and New Year's. But it doesn't need fixing. I simply disconnected it."

Neal looked at me with astonishment. "You what?"

I looked back at him calmly, "I am trying to write a grant. I need to concentrate, so I disconnected the phone."

Neal looked at me with mock displeasure, "Here I am, trying for half an hour to call you and invite you to come to the lab to have a piece of Tania's birthday cake, and you go and disconnect the phone. I should go back and eat your piece for you. Come on, everyone's waiting."

I followed Neal back to the lab. Ken was preparing coffee in the hallway and Tania was cutting slabs of cake for us all. Even Opera-Singh was there, praising the appearance of Tania's homemade cake. For some reason, Opera-Singh was still unusually pleasant to Tania; perhaps that was because there hadn't yet been any competition between them for lab equipment. I was shrewd enough to know that this could change very quickly, and Tania was aware of this too. Yet she herself was more than pleasant to Opera-Singh.

Tania passed out her homemade apple cake on paper plates, and Ken made himself useful serving mugs of coffee to us all. He was a man of action, preferring performance rather than the uneasiness of having to speak. It seemed to me that everyone was waiting for me to break the ice.

"With treats like this, it's too bad you don't have birthdays more often," I said to Tania.

"Here, here," Neal agreed between mouthfuls, "this is great cake." It was clear that Neal was enjoying the cake.

"This cake definitely has the correct balance of spicing," pronounced Opera-Singh rather unexpectedly. He was not one to pass compliments off easily.

"Didn't you invite the Smitherians over to celebrate, too?" I chided Neal and Tania.

Professor Lewis Smithers had the largest lab in the department, with about seven Ph.D. students and three or four other postdoctoral workers. We all referred to anyone who worked in his lab as a "Smitherian." Neal claimed that the main characteristic that dominated all the Smitherians was a combination of arrogance mixed with a superiority complex. In my view, this diagnosis more or less hit the nail on the head. It was true that Lewis Smithers was an excellent scientist, but he certainly had a way of first choosing arrogant students and later actually building up their developing superiority complexes. It was not a healthy situation. His students seemed to view themselves as an exceptional little clique of extremely qualified scientists, with whom no other lab inside or outside of the department could compete. In addition, Smithers apparently drilled into their already inflated heads the idea that *their* research was by far the most important research done in the entire department. The severity of this problem was further enhanced by the fact that Smithers would take on many students who would go on to begin a direct Ph.D. program, without the necessity of doing a master's degree first. This would further inflate the egos of these young students, without giving them a chance to see what science was like in any other lab outside of Smithers' tightly ruled domain. It would take many of his former students years of adjustment, after they had finally finished their doctorates, to realize that science existed outside the walls of Smithers' labs. Unfortunately, even for some of the talented ones, that would be too late.

Neal piped up quickly, "That's okay, they've taken over the department library now for their weekly group meeting. Better check that all the journals don't disappear when they leave the library afterwards."

We did not have our own group meetings very frequently. Since we were "lean" and perhaps "mean" (as many departmental colleagues would complain of Opera-Singh and sometimes of Neal), we did not need these meetings as a formal way to update each other on progress. Aside from that, for all his diligence at work, Opera-Singh was not quick at comprehending the research of others. It seemed to me that whenever we, as a lab, would sit together to discuss each other's results, even informally, Opera-Singh would keep asking very basic questions, force us to go way back, and limit any progress in these discussions. After two exhausting hours, we would find that no one really benefited from these meetings. It was easier to have separate talks; sometimes I met with Neal, Tania, and Ken, but without Opera-Singh. And Opera-Singh certainly didn't mind; he hated these talks. They took up his valuable work time and delayed his departure from the lab in the evening. He was anxious to get home to his plants.

I stayed for a few minutes longer with my charges, praising Tania's delicious cake and joking that her husband, Michael, was lucky to be married to such a talented baker. Tania blushed lightly, but took my comment with her natural good taste. She was now twenty-eight years old, and she had been married to Michael for more than three years. That's certainly longer than my marriage with Jeannie had lasted or, for that matter, longer than any of my subsequent relationships. It was now almost 5:30 in the afternoon, and I headed back to my office to finish dealing with various administrative issues. First I scanned and deleted eighty-seven of the ninety-six e-mails in my inbox. E-mail correspondence, requests, institutional safety exams, radioactive material, and animals-in-research exams were beginning to take a serious toll on my available time. I efficiently dispatched with my required duties, wished my fellow workers a good evening, and prepared to set out for the day. Neal looked at me with that smug smile of his. Sometimes I felt that I could hit him when he looked like that. "Aren't you forgetting something?" he asked me with that faked innocence of his.

"What, Neal?" I was too tired to try and figure out what he wanted.

"You forgot to remind us to lock the doors, shut off the gas, turn off the centrifuges, and all that," Neal said wistfully. Neal was almost always last in the lab in the evening and I certainly had no qualms about his responsible nature. I would hear many complaints about Neal over the years, but being apathetic or irresponsible was not among them. Nevertheless, I did have this habit of reminding him to close up properly.

"Maybe it's about time I gave you a chance to see if I can trust you," I needled him as I stroked my beard, and we all laughed. But we all laughed for our own different reasons.

The elevators were still out of service, so I plodded down the stairs, trying to remember where I had parked my car that morning. It seemed like days ago. Was this the start of my memory fading? Dementia? Alzheimer's? Or was I just tired from the stress at the lab? The developmental neurologists liked to lecture about what they called "plasticity" of the brain—the ability of the brain to adapt and go with the flow. However, this plasticity apparently only exists when the individual is young. I must have no plasticity left, I thought. Even if I did, these plastic neural connections would probably freeze and crack in the icy Ontario winters. I forced myself to concentrate on the stairs. The lights went out automatically at 5:30 in the evening, and this left our institute, stairways included, in the dark during the cool autumns and long Ontario winters. There was a push-button light switch hooked to a timer at the entrance to every floor, but I found that although I was in reasonable shape from the running that I still do from time to time, the light would shut off inevitably by the fifth or sixth step—and this was going down. Neal had once suggested another of his many famous tricks—sticking a match in the push-button light switch to keep the timer on. But I couldn't be bothered, and, anyway, I didn't smoke. I found myself wondering again how the older professors managed. Were they all in great shape? Did they all have night vision goggles? Did they all smoke and carry matches? What kind of scientific institute was this anyway? I must stop this, I resolved. I'm starting to think like Neal again.

I managed to locate my car in the faculty parking lot without too much trouble. Some evenings my deteriorating memory led me to search frantically for my car for several minutes, worrying that it had been stolen. It was cold out, "nippy" as we used to say of those chilly evenings in Saskatchewan, and I was glad to get in the car and get the heater going. I had always been a lover of summer, in Saskatchewan or in Ontario, but I could take the icy winters too. What really "took the piss out of me," as my British mate Nigel would say, were the transformations from one season to the next. I suppose that even after all those years, my exposure to the ups and downs of dad's bipolar disorder would render me weary of any change—even in the weather.

When I finally got home, carrying a few light bags of groceries, I was almost amazed to note that the elevator in my apartment building was actually in service. What a treat. There's nothing like my institute to allow one to enjoy the finer pleasures of life. As I slid the key into my apartment door, I could already hear Compo scratching away at it from the inside. I steeled myself for the greeting; Compo loved me, but that wouldn't stop him from practically castrating me if I didn't turn my body sideways upon entering the apartment. He was not a large dog; in fact he looked a lot larger than he really was because of his thick coat of winter fur. However, he was just tall enough when stretched out upon his hind legs to reach my vital parts. The most potentially dangerous occasions were the ones when I came home carrying bags from the supermarket; I didn't have time to properly defend myself. However, this evening I managed to avoid any damage. I even thought wistfully that, if things were to work out tonight in a certain progressive manner, it would have been a difficult thing to explain to a first time date: "I'm awfully sorry, but, uh, my dog sort of hit a sore spot. Perhaps we'll have to take a rain check. I'm in a bit of pain." Would any woman believe me? Would Julia believe me? I found myself starting to feel guilt at the thought of going out on a date with some other woman, even a casual date, when I was so obviously attracted to Julia. Too late now, I thought to myself, I'd better shower and call Jim.

A visit to the Maple Leaf Gardens to see the Toronto Maple Leafs in action, followed by some Mexican food, was Jim's idea. Although I liked to watch the odd hockey game, preferably avoiding the smoky arena by following on television, I was not much of a fan. Still, anything was better than the opera. I knew that both Jim and Carol followed the hockey season avidly, and hoped for all our sakes that my date, whose name I learned was Duffy, would not be too bored with the game.

Since Jim and Carol lived on the other side of town, not too far from Duffy's apartment, we decided to meet at the arena, coming in separate cars. I was to join the three of them just outside the ticket counter. I stood alone by the ticket window, feeling guilty at abandoning my grant application together with Julia for this date. I shivered slightly, watching the vivid antics of the ticket hawkers on the steps, desperately trying to unload their extra seats at a profit. After all, tonight the Montreal Canadiens were here to play, in a battle for first place. I pulled my scarf around my neck more tightly, waiting for Jim and company, and was reminded of a very different hockey arena many years ago.

CHAPTER THREE

I couldn't have been more than ten or eleven years old during the cold, icy winter when mom and dad decided to take a February holiday and fly off to the Grand Cayman Islands. This was the first time that they had ever left us alone, I later realized, because this was one of the rare stretches where dad had actually been feeling well long enough to plan such a vacation. Ervin was particularly excited about the upcoming three weeks. "We can stay up as late as we like every night and make crank phone calls. I'm going to let the Taylors have it. They'll be sorry they ever messed with Ervin Miller!"

Although Ervin was only eight or nine years old at the time, he would never forgive our rather unpleasant next-door neighbors for calling the police that time when he had played his toy trumpet out in the back yard at four in the morning. Cindy, who was only six years old, apparently did not fully comprehend the situation. It was difficult, if not impossible, for her to imagine three whole weeks without seeing mom. She looked forward to the promise of presents that she expected our parents to bring for her when they came home from their trip. Mom had sat me down and explained how important this trip could be for dad—the vacation might help him stay happy for a prolonged period of time—so I felt glad that she and dad were going away. I knew that I would miss mom especially, but I was old enough to understand that three weeks were really not all that long. Little did I know how eternal those weeks would actually seem. When mom explained the situation to me, she had not yet divulged her plan for leaving us in the care of a "professional woman." I had been certain that we would be entrusted to Grandpa Joe's capable and loving care. To this day still I cannot comprehend why they didn't leave us with Grandpa Joe. I suspect that even back then, long before the major rift between mom and Grandpa Joe, there was already a tense and suspicion-filled relationship between the two of them. Their opposing wills were tugging them apart inevitably, like tectonic plates. And dad was the city of Los Angeles or San Francisco, where all the faults accrued and all the destruction occurred.

In those days, although Grandpa Joe did not yet live with us officially on a permanent basis, he spent much of his available time at our home, helping out. To me it seemed perfectly logical for him to move in with us for three weeks until mom and dad returned. In fact, as I later learned, Grandpa Joe was severely insulted by the lack of confidence in him. I think that mom wanted to prevent him from securing a permanent foothold in our house; she was afraid that they would return from their vacation to find that the entire household was totally dependent on Grandpa Joe. For mom, whose training played such a major role in her life, it must have been analogous to giving antibiotics when there was no bacterial infection in the throat. The unnecessary use of these drugs only served to induce resistant bacterial strains that were eventually much harder to get rid of. But mom categorically denied such ideas in conversations that we had recently. Regardless, Grandpa Joe would never believe my mother's version of the story, her claims that she didn't want to 'push the children' on him. It's certainly true that he would never have refused, whatever he thought of the idea. But he definitely would have been in favor of the idea in the first place and would have gladly stayed with us during those few weeks. At any rate, for whatever reason, mom and dad opted for a "professional woman," a woman who earned her keep by moving from family to family to take care of children while their parents were away on vacation. Those three weeks with Ms. Telia Mastpole would supply the three of us with unpleasant dreams and vivid memories of her eccentric behavior for years to come.

Ms. Mastpole was a most domineering presence. She must have been in her early fifties, and those fifty-odd years sufficed for her to accumulate and support a rather massive frame. Ervin, although still too young to be interested in girls at the time, nevertheless managed to note with a smirk that she possessed "steel knockers." I sent him to check his hockey puck collection, to make sure that she wasn't padding her chest with his sentimentally valuable hockey pucks. He took my suggestion literally, of course, and ran to his room to ensure that the collection remained intact. Ms. Mastpole, or Ms. Telia, as she later besieged upon us to call her, had her own peculiar manner of dressing. She made her grand entrance, flopping awkwardly out of my parents' room each morning, attired in distinctly tattered and badly stretched leopard-patterned tights, several sizes too small for her wide rump, and a tight, brightly colored pullover sweater. It seemed to me that her attempts at early morning fashion were, at best, wasted on Ervin and me, not to mention little Cindy. One Saturday morning Ervin and I were sitting across from each other at the kitchen breakfast table, still half asleep, when Ms. Telia appeared in her usual garish costume. I leaned over to Ervin and whispered rather rudely, "Is she planning on going to the zoo?"

Ms. Telia, whose auditory skills could already have benefited from a hearing aid and were heading south rapidly, managed to pick out the word "zoo." "You kids wanna go to the zoo?"

"Stevie does," Ervin piped up before I could get in a good swift kick under the table.

"What Ervin means," I said interpreting hastily, while flashing a dangerous look at Ervin, now obviously in pain from my kick, "is that I'd like to go but have a basketball practice. Maybe Cindy would like to go."

By this time, I had already become a very independent child. My family's unfortunate situation had forced me to learn to take care of myself. Mom had even left me a fair amount of cash to pick up food at the corner store or buy whatever I thought was necessary. She had enough foresight to realize that I might not put my trust in Ms. Telia. I walked to school in the mornings, with Ervin and Cindy trailing along, or bundled us all onto the bus at the corner bus stop if it was really cold out. After school, on many afternoons I played with my friends, usually going directly to their homes, which were often within walking distance. Even with dad on vacation, I still did not feel comfortable having my friends come over because of Ms. Telia. I was deeply embarrassed by her, but in a different way than the embarrassment dad caused me. With dad, I wanted to avoid the uncomfortable and awkward feeling that my friends might encounter seeing how sorry dad looked some of the time; I did not want them to pity me. With Ms. Telia, I was frankly embarrassed at the thought that my friends would laugh and poke fun at me. I also played basketball on the school team, with several practices a week after school and at least one game. On weekends, I would meet my friends downtown at the Y for activities that were always sports related. Sometimes on Saturdays, I would even take the bus to the central library downtown to pick out a few new books if mom or Grandpa Joe hadn't supplied me with enough reading material. I was beginning to tire of Grandpa Joe's nonstop praise of Adam Smith's *The Wealth of Nations* and his passion for Ayn Rand's objectivist ideology. And mom didn't always find the time to help me choose good literature; she herself had been reading less and less in recent years. Actually, if it hadn't been for Ervin and Cindy, I could have managed fine by myself, provided that there were no unexpected problems with the house or anything out of the ordinary to deal with. Anyway, Grandpa Joe was always available, and he didn't live too far away.

One evening, after Cindy and Ervin had finally gone to bed, I stood alone in the kitchen preparing my lunch for the next day. Ms. Telia sidled up beside me and asked, "What does Ervin like in his sandwich for lunch?"

Pitying Ervin this time, I answered truthfully, "He doesn't like tuna, but he eats practically everything else."

Unlike Ervin and Cindy, I had been making my own sandwiches and choosing my own seasonal fruit for my school lunches for several years now. On the way home from school, the next afternoon, Ervin asked me, "Hey Stevie, what kind of sandwich did you get for lunch today?"

"I didn't get any sandwich," I answered haughtily. "You forget, Ervin, that I make my own sandwiches. If you weren't so spoiled lazy, you should try it yourself. I made myself a tuna salad sandwich for lunch today."

"Yuck!" said Ervin automatically. "But I'd even prefer tuna," he lamented. "This meat in my sandwich is disgusting." He opened his lunch box and pulled out the uneaten sandwich. "What is it, anyway?" he asked me suspiciously.

"I'm not sure, Ervin," I said, taking a quick whiff. My sense of smell had always been particularly developed. One spring I had even shocked Grandpa Joe by telling him that I smelled a batch of his famous chocolate chip cookies from the end of the street on the way home from school. "It may be a pork product, possibly ham."

"But that's not kosher," Ervin decreed.

"You eat pepperoni pizzas and cheeseburgers, and you like bacon and eggs. What are you going on about 'kosher' for?"

"But this is different—it's *pork*," he said with an intonation of disgust that I can still hear today.

"Come on Ervin, you'd probably like it more than Grandpa Joe's tuna sandwiches. Give me a break."

But Ervin could be extremely stubborn, and no amount of convincing could get him, at his age, to try the "unclean" pork product. One thing was certain, if mom or even Grandpa Joe had

41

prepared the sandwich for him, Ervin would have wolfed it down lovingly without a second thought.

I don't think that it would be a fair assessment of the situation to say that the major complications that ensued between Ms. Telia and my family were in the sphere of religion. It wasn't a matter of Jewish versus Christian upbringing or even some more refined differences connected with religious affairs or practices. We were not a religious family. Our Jewishness was expressed in a secular nature, mainly by family connection. We also felt a common horror at the nightmare of the holocaust with its ghastly gas chambers and shared an appreciation of the State of Israel as a sort of insurance factor against any recurrence of mass violence against Jews. However, from a practical, day-to-day standpoint, there was really very little that could be recognized as "a Jewish lifestyle," with the possible exception of the secular Jewish day school that we attended. That, too, was a debatable point. Our school had such a good reputation that there were at least as many non-Jews as Jews who attended. Along with us, they were happily learning some Hebrew, not exactly a useful second language to say the least, but certainly not damaging. No, the differences between Ms. Telia and ourselves could be more accurately described as cultural ones. Truthfully, in retrospect I can say that some of these were due to some simple snobbery that was present in our upbringing. My family had never been interested in garage sales, basement bargains, cheap clothes, or second-hand cutlery. Up until that point in our perhaps sheltered lives, we had not suffered from a lack of any possessions. We were not a wealthy family, but we did belong to the "upper middle class." However, poor Ms. Telia couldn't pass up any of these bargain events. Each Saturday and Sunday, she would cart poor Cindy around the city, from garage to garage and basement to basement, looking for bargains. Ervin was convinced that she wanted to change her image: "Maybe she's looking for some racoon pants. Those tiger things are looking pretty mangy." Even for his age, Ervin had always had his own very unusual, but stingingly articulate manner of expression. He still tends to speak this way, despite retaining a rather significant weakness in communication skills. Mom maintains that the skills are actually present, but dormant. As usual, I don't particularly have much faith in mom's judgment in these matters, and I have continuously recommended that someone get Ervin to see a psychologist many times over the years, but always to no avail.

One evening, several days after our parents had flown off to their Grand Cayman winter vacation, I began to sense a widening in the tremendous rift that already lay between Ms. Telia Mastpole, me, Ervin, and even little Cindy. It was a dark, bitterly cold, Saturday evening, and I had just returned by bus from the Y downtown, where I had played floor hockey in the gym all afternoon. I hadn't properly dried my hair in the locker room before setting out home and this was a bad mistake. During the short walk home from the bus stop, I had accumulated little tufts of ice rooted to the base of my hair follicles, which had formed even under my woolen hat. Ms. Telia opened the door and panicked immediately.

"You'll catch the death of you going out like that in the winter. I'm going to prepare you a lemon-tea concoction. You must drink it. If you don't, the devil knows what may happen. It's dangerous to go out with wet hair."

I tried politely to refuse, arguing smoothly that a few minutes beside the radiator would warm me up. I hated tea. I hated lemon tea even more. I shuddered at the thought of what the "concoction" part would add to this drink that I already despised. She probably keeps bottles of cat spittle or fetal skunk protein for these occasions, I thought airily. But at that point I could see no other way out. In fact, I knew that Ms. Telia really only wanted to help, in her own way. She was even missing part of her televangelist prayer meeting on TV to prepare the horrid tea for me. What could I do?

With the nauseating concoction steaming in my hand, I promised to try and drink it. It reeked of some other unfamiliar herbs, reminding me of the odors of a dentist's office. I had visions of Dr. Middleton with his rubber gloves, and "open wide," and the whine of his drill. I could picture the suction straw used to dry my mouth when I would inevitably gag. I sat there feeling sorry for myself and finally began assessing my options. One possibility was simply to try and drink it. I considered trying to swallow it all in one go. But the concoction was boiling hot. I'd only end up burning my tongue and throat. If I tried to sip it and then vomited, she would probably force a number of even worse concoctions on me to stop the nausea. That thought was especially frightening. I began to sweat profusely. At that age, I didn't know what palpitations were, but I could definitely feel my heart beating rapidly. There seemed no way out, no easy escape, and I could smell that horrid concoction still steaming away in my hands, a continuous reminder of my troubled situation. I hoped that Ms. Telia would get up and go off to the toilet or become distracted with a phone call. That way I could at least quickly poison one of the plants in the room—better it than me. But lady luck was not smiling down on me. I tried to take a sip of the awful smelling fluid—I really did try—and nearly retched. Ms. Telia looked at me and said, "Come on, bottoms up, and down it goes. You're not leaving this room until you drink it all up."

Suddenly I had a brilliant idea. Thinking back on my ingenious brainwave, I become angry when I hear of complaints today that scientists lack originality and are noncreative. Ms. Telia's televangelist program had ended, but the weekly *Bingo* had begun. She spread out her arsenal of bingo forms, purchased at the local lottery office, in preparation of winning this evening's game. I hoped that the supreme intellectual effort of tracing down those numbers and circling them carefully with her red pen just might supply the necessary distraction for me to execute my plan. Although I wasn't facing the television set, I heard the monotone voice of the announcer drone on, "Under the B, fifteen, under the B, fifteen." He repeated each number three or four times. He sounded distinctly bored with himself. I guess the intellectual level of the people who participated in Saturday evening Channel Three *Bingo* was known to him. Cautiously, I peeked to my left and saw that Ms. Telia was becoming more and more involved in her game. I desperately hoped that this would allow me to carry out my plan. The necessity of following several cards simultaneously was apparently a challenge even for someone with her years of bingo experience. Nevertheless, she cast a quick glance at me and ordered, "Come on, drink up."

"Sure," I agreed amiably. There was little sense in raising her suspicions, so I played for time. "But it's still so hot. I'll let it cool down a little first."

"When the commercials come on, I'll get you some ice," she promised.

Every five minutes or so, the nauseating commercials appeared. They were especially adapted to the Saturday evening bingo crowd—mostly attempts to sell cheap kitchen gadgets and old Elvis or country records that could be bought over the phone NOW with a valid credit card number. If the concoction didn't do me in, I thought pessimistically, Elvis certainly will.

The NOW from the commercial meant to me "now or never." This was my only chance. I reached cautiously over to the decorative glass coffee table and managed to grab a blue Lladró vase and slide it onto the chair beside me. Ms. Telia was still absorbed with *Bingo* and I could hear the witless announcer ramble on, "Under the G, fifty-one, under the G, fifty-one." Without looking at Ms. Telia, I slowly began to empty the steaming mug of horrible smelling liquid into the Lladró vase. It looked like a perfect fit. I took a final fake swig from the mug, and said, "Thanks, Ms. Telia, I drank it all."

"Good for you," she muttered, circling N43 as she spoke.

My next problem was to slide the Lladró vase back into its place on the coffee table. This was slightly more difficult than I had anticipated, because the vase was extremely hot and very difficult to pick up. Eventually, with much patience and coordinated manual dexterity, I managed to wrap my shirt sleeve around it and gradually slide it back to its original position. However, my silent sigh of relief was premature. Like many things in life that revolve in phases from good to bad, the interim periods of normalcy are often too short to allow a full appreciation of the period of respite. From the corner of my eye, I could see steam rising from the top of the vase. I should have acted immediately, but another thing that I have learned over the years is that people often hope for the best—that things will improve or go away without any intervention. Both mom and Grandpa Joe seemed to sport that type of attitude, at least in their day-to-day actions and with respect to dad's condition. From my own experience, things don't necessarily improve; they often fester and deteriorate, and often it's too late to do anything at a later stage. That's exactly what happened to the poor Lladró vase. It boiled and bubbled and steamed and frothed until finally, with a noise that sounded like the cracking of a Ping-Pong ball after a hard hit spike, simply disintegrated into thousands of tiny pieces, with the nauseating steamy liquid lolling about the coffee table like lava overflowing from an active volcano. Ms. Telia would later have to retrieve her bingo results from her sister on the phone. In the meantime, she sent me off to my room—"With no dinner for you, young man!"—extremely upset with me for lying to her and trying to "cheat her." I had no qualms about going to do penance in my room. I was very sorry about the vase (who would have expected it to be unable to withstand the heat), but I was very hungry. I had come home from a full day of floor hockey and was absolutely ravenous. I was well known to my friends and family for my particularly healthy appetite. I had no intention of fasting; I didn't even fast on Yom Kippur, the Jewish Day of Atonement. There was no way that Ms. Telia was going to force me to fast.

Sitting on my bed I contemplated the situation and the strategic options available. It was seven p.m. and I was famished. I knew that I could simply disobey Ms. Telia, walk into the kitchen, and make myself some dinner. The odds were that she wouldn't physically try to stop a child from eating. However, I thought to myself, she *was* physically capable of forcing me back to my room. She obviously weighed two or three times more than me, and I didn't relish the thought of getting into a wrestling match with her. Also, this was only the second week since mom and dad had left. Who knew how badly things could degenerate in the final week? What might she try to do to me? Another option was to call Grandpa Joe and ask him to intervene. He would be very understanding. The problem, I realized, was that Ms. Telia would see that as an undermining of her authority, and that might make matters even worse. I did not want to cause Grandpa Joe any more anguish than he already felt. What else could I do? I flipped through my wallet and found that I still had lots of money left. I also had more put away that both mom and Grandpa Joe had given me. I decided to gamble. I left the lights and the radio on in my room. I piled some cushions under the heavy winter quilt, to make it look as though I was asleep on the bed, and locked the door from the inside, to ensure that Ms. Telia wouldn't be able to snoop. I could easily ply my bedroom lock open from the outside with the kitchen scissors, something that Ervin often did to incite me. I slid the door closed quietly, took one of dad's old jackets from the back hallway and slid out the back door into the dark, cold street. Ten minutes later I was sitting in Donovan's Pizza after having ordered a large pizza and Caesar salad. Since Ms. Telia's arrival, I had sorely missed our traditional family salads. Ms. Telia was a believer in cooked vegetables, steamed peas and carrots, but she never prepared fresh salads for us. When I had finished my leisurely dinner, I walked another few blocks over to the community center library and spent a couple hours doing some quiet reading. Even back then, books had always had a tremendous ability to calm me. After delaying as long as possible, I finally set out for home in the chilly night, debating, as I approached the driveway, whether I should come in the back or front door. I could see that Ms. Telia was still up watching television in the den; it was early and she was quite a night bird. I realized that she would hear me whichever door

I entered. Suddenly I had a bold new idea. I walked around the back to the garage and removed dad's old coat, his snow boots, and the rest of the outdoor garb. It was freezing cold, but I could foresee a way that might lead me out of trouble. In my socks, I slid over to the wooden gate, which was the entrance to our back yard, and propped it open. Then I retraced my steps to the back door, quickly unlocked it and shouted out into the darkness from where I had just come, "Hey, you, get away from there. I'm calling the police!"

Ms. Telia ran to the back door in a flash, evidently quite alarmed. "What's going on?" she asked with a touch of hysteria, breathing sharply.

There I was, with no jacket on, only in my socks standing at the back door, just as though I had spent the entire evening in my room. Although my bedroom door was closed, it was easy to see that the lights in my room and the radio were still on. "I heard some noise out in the back. Someone opened the back gate, I saw his shadow!" I whispered to her.

"Did you see who it was?" she questioned me.

"No, but as soon as I got to the back door and shouted out he ran off back through the gate."

"Well, there's not much point in calling the police now, I suppose. Whoever it was is probably long gone by now."

I couldn't help agreeing with Ms. Telia this time, in one of the rare instances where we saw eye to eye. Point counterpoint, I thought to myself, recalling one of my favorites of Huxley's work. I must not forget to retrieve dad's jacket and boots from the garage tomorrow morning.

However, Ms. Telia's influence on me was really quite minimal compared to her effect on little Cindy. Just learning to read, Cindy automatically integrated Ms. Telia's attitude towards all walks of life, sucking up her being like a sponge. In just two weeks, Cindy had become a bubble gum junkie. Ervin joked that she couldn't pass up a gumball machine without investing a minor fortune in it. There was much truth to this. Ms. Telia's favorable attitude to bingo, lotteries, and such legitimate gambling seemed to have Cindy hooked. Cindy would help Ms. Telia spread out her multitude of bingo cards and cheer her on when her chances looked good. But Ms. Telia never won. At least not while she stayed with us.

However, far more frightening was Cindy's potentially damaging attachment to the televangelist shows. Even months after Ms. Telia had disappeared from our lives, Cindy still spent many hours watching the televangelists on TV. Their power and sheer confidence held an animal type of magnetism for her. Ms. Telia had Cindy hooked, and it would take months of careful psychological attempts to eventually unhook her. I once made the mistake of trying to ask Ms. Telia to watch her televangelists in dad's room, but she rebuffed my request immediately. "Let Cindy decide for herself. The Good Lord has the power and no harm can come from following Him." I think that what partly "cured" Cindy was Roy Winston, the chief televangelist himself, who urged his followers, young Cindy among them, "to dig deep into your pockets for the Good Lord." Cindy dug deep alright, but as Ervin would claim, she wasn't willing to dig deep enough for the Good Lord. She needed the contents of her pockets for those bubble gum machines.

While Ms. Telia probably had the most lasting impression upon poor little Cindy, and while I managed to slyly navigate my way around Ms. Telia's influence, Ervin by far had the most trouble.

Ervin was, at the best of times, a professional "bug." Mom used to say that he could drive an elephant crazy. With Ms. Telia around, I didn't know about elephants, but I had no doubt regarding tigers or leopards. Ervin had always been very forward, at times even quite rude, and was not afraid of being sent off to his room. To prepare for these frequent emergencies, he had a secret stock of food hidden in his closet. He would not go hungry when Ms. Telia sent him to his room, which was practically every evening. I can't even remember the reasons for these daily punishments. Once, I think, he put Cindy's underpants on his head and went wandering around the house like that. Another time, Ms. Telia sent him to his room for continually "repeating the name of the Lord in vain." That evening, I also nearly got sent to my room for commenting that the televangelists should also be sent to *their* rooms for the same reason. I think that I was only spared my own punishment because Ms. Telia didn't quite understand what I meant.

Perhaps the most frightening incident with Ervin was the time that he began swearing and cursing the televangelists. He was absolutely enraged, and I don't know what induced his burst of anger at the time. To this day, I cannot recall ever seeing Ervin so angry, so hysterically out of control. Ms. Telia acted imme-diately, grabbing Ervin by the earlobe and dragging him to the washroom. Ervin was yelling at the top of his voice, "Fuck the Good Lord. Screw the Reverend Roy Winston; he sucks hockey pucks." Ms. Telia managed to stuff Ervin into the bath, using her bulk to sit on him, pry open his mouth and shove a small bar of soap into it. Ervin screamed and shouted, cursing the "Good Lord" more and more, choking and retching on the vile soap. I was utterly powerless. The only thing I could do was to call Ms. Telia to the phone (although no one had actually called) giving Ervin a chance to escape and lock himself in his room. But Ervin was made of strong stuff. A little soap couldn't slow him down. That night, he hid a walkie-talkie under mom and dad's bed where Ms. Telia slept, leaving it on in the receiving mode. He set his alarm clock for three a.m. and proceeded to harass Ms. Telia all night remotely from the other receiver of his walkie-talkie set, turning it on "transmit" and whispering "Fuck the Good Lord." I don't think she ever discovered where that came from; she must have chalked it up to blasphemous dreams.

It wasn't until sometime during the third week of my parents' winter vacation that we were actually able to finally rid ourselves of Ms. Telia's tiger-like clutch once and for all. Unfortunately, this was not easily accomplished—not without a lot of pain, es-pecially on Ervin's behalf. One afternoon after school, Ervin and

I moved the outdoor ball hockey nets down into the basement. We waited until Ms. Telia was busy on the phone, explaining to her sister the remarkable technique she had used to avoid having a black cat cross her path that morning. Little did she comprehend the vast multitude of occurrences other than black cats crossing one's path that could be messengers of ill-fated luck. We closed the door leading down to the basement, our infamous "hockey arena," and began to play one-on-one hockey, with the two nets as our goals. Ervin was very much influenced by the "hooligans" or "goons," as they were known in hockey circles. They were these huge, skating "bodyguards," who were not all that mobile and lacked any talent whatsoever. However, their ominously formidable appearance was certainly enough to get the point across. Occasionally they would be involved in huge brawls on the ice; more often they would actually instigate them. Many of the newer American fans enjoyed watching these goons; many of them didn't yet understand the beauty of ice hockey, and the goons served as another form of wrestling on ice. At any rate, Ervin often tried to imitate the antics of these overweight lugs, and for this reason he would try colliding with me in the basement with his plastic hockey stick dangling dangerously above his head. "Ervin," I would complain, "get your stick down, you'll poke out my eye."

"Just play the game," Ervin would retort. "If you can't take the rough stuff, go play dolls with Cindy."

Eventually, our hockey match would turn into a bit of a roughhouse; this was part Ervin's fault and part mine. As the older, and theoretically more responsible, brother, I really should have stopped and gone to play dolls with Cindy, but I didn't feel that Ervin was exactly in a qualified position to threaten me. I was also too stubborn to give in. Ultimately, things got a little out of hand and I ended up "dumping" Ervin into the "boards" with a resounding cross-check. Down he went, favoring his left ankle, swearing away, "Fuck the Good Lord. Fuck the Good Lord." When I finally managed to haul Ervin up the stairs and get him into the den, Ms. Telia took a good look at the swollen ankle and diagnosed, "It's nothing—just a light sprain. Poppycock." She liked that stupid expression. Ms. Telia set out to find the proper herbs to set on poor Ervin's ankle, and he lay there in much pain, muttering to himself "Fuck the Good Lord." I casually suggested that maybe we had better take Ervin in to the hospital to have a doctor look at him, but Ms. Telia wouldn't have any of that. "Poppycock," she said again, more than doubling my own irritation. "All he needs are some wintergreen and jasmine potions. Here, help me put these on his ankle."

However, when Ervin began whimpering that night long after midnight, I began to fret. I knew Ervin, and I knew that he had a tremendous ability to withstand physical pain—far greater than my own. If he couldn't sleep, then I knew we needed a doctor. I called up Grandpa Joe and within twenty minutes he had come to pick us up and take us down to the emergency room at the hospital. Ms. Telia was livid at the undermining of her authority. Grandpa Joe was enraged by her lack of responsibility. When we finally came home from the hospital, with Ervin's ankle set in a cast, Grandpa Joe had had enough of Ms. Telia. I will never know exactly what he said to her or how he got her out of the house so quickly, but thankfully that was the last we ever saw of her.

CHAPTER FOUR

I t was a cool mid-November evening as I stood uneasily outside the ticket office in front of Maple Leaf Gardens, waiting for my good friend Jim, his wife Carol, and her mysterious friend. I knew in advance that this friend was another one of a long series of failed attempts to fix me up with someone. This someone, I was soon to learn, had a small earring running through her nose and called herself Duffy.

Fortunately, I did not have to wait too long for the threesome to arrive, as I was not dressed appropriately for the bitterly cool evening. I was not wearing a hat or gloves but only a thin wool scarf wrapped around my neck. I was beginning to feel my ears cooling rapidly and could imagine them turning that bright pinkish color so typical of partly frostbitten skin. Chilly winds were whipping blue colored papers around by the stairs where I waited patiently. I realized later that they were advertisements for an enterprising new Italian restaurant, and that they had been pegged to the windshields of the cars parked in the arena parking lot. Ironically, these advertisements were printed on recycled paper and had the cute little smiley face in the corner of the page that was supposed to symbolize "environmental friendliness," whatever that meant. Not very much, I thought, since these papers were now floating around and littering all of downtown

Toronto. At this point, my toes joined in and also began to send warning signals to my brain concerning their increasing numbness. I wiggled my jacket sleeve up a little to glance at my watch and found that it was still early. Almost simultaneously I spotted Jim and Carol coming my way together with a rather tall woman sporting a small funny hat placed strategically in the center of her long, wavy blonde hair. Jim was one of my oldest friends, way back from my high school days in Regina. We had arrived in Toronto roughly at the same time and had even shared a flat together while studying at the University of Toronto in our undergraduate years. Those were good times for us both, despite the difficulties that we each had financially, especially Jim. Now Jim was extremely busy working for one of the leading architectural firms in the city. Even though we didn't manage to spend much time together anymore, we still remained close friends. My marriage to Jeannie, which hadn't lasted very long, had probably induced the first real rift between us. Jim and I had been playing tennis together on Friday afternoons ever since our high school days back in Regina. When I first began living with Jeannie, she never tried to interfere with our weekly tennis matches. I'm not exactly sure why, but after we got married, things changed. Somehow these tennis meetings began to intimidate her. She had never really liked Jim and always maintained that he was boring. She also made no special efforts to hide her feelings towards him. Jeannie must have been bothered by what I might potentially disclose to Jim about her or about her relationship with me. I had no way of knowing this for sure, but all my intuition led me to believe this was so. Undoubtedly, Jeannie felt betrayed by my closeness with Jim. Her weekly pouting every Friday when I announced that I was off to play tennis with Jim was not a display of apathy. I knew Jeannie well enough to understand that she would never say why these meetings bothered her. She wouldn't even have admitted that that they did. But despite her unwillingness to broach the subject, I was certain that she considered the tennis as an excuse for me to gossip with Jim. This only highlights the tremendous lack of communication that characterized our relationship. For some reason, it never occurred to me at the time to actually *ask* her what the problem was. I had never been the radically tight-lipped, secret service type that typified Jeannie's social persona even among friends. Still, no one who knew me could possibly have imagined that I would speak of my private feelings and affairs. I was a dry, wrinkled scientist, more likely to discuss test tubes than my sex life or relationship with my wife. On occasions where *some* human interest was called for, at the most I would pull a few stories of Compo the dog from out of my sleeve. That was about as far as I would go. Obviously, her concerns were ridiculous. I never told Jim anything about my relationship with Jeannie. On the other hand, Jim didn't hesitate to unload stories of his own complicated relationships, especially a particularly awkward and difficult one with a married woman. I served partly as friend and partly as adviser. I felt like a father confessor some Fridays. However, I never disclosed to Jeannie the contents of my private talks with Jim; perhaps that's what incited her suspicions and anger.

The second rift between Jim and me occurred sometime after he had begun living with Carol. Although Carol was very friendly towards me, and even very supportive, I still felt very uneasy in her presence. As opposed to Jeannie, she had no qualms regarding my friendship with Jim. Carol arrived on the scene at the time when I was still struggling to get my personal life back together again after my rather traumatic separation from Jeannie. Not that my personal life is "altogether together" right now, but at least comparatively speaking, Carol and I first became acquainted during one of the more difficult periods of my adult life. Despite my ability to eventually move on with my life in the aftermath of my painful divorce, Carol would continue to treat me as "poor Steve," never letting up with those sympathetic poses. She did not do this to spite me but out of genuine affection and willingness to help me. But as is often the case, especially in the world of science, what counts is the end result. And in this case, the end product was that too much of Carol could drive me batty, or as my friend Nigel would say "lead to my derailment." Those British could cheer me up just by talking and using their brilliant expressions. God bless the Queen and her ice lollies, and Princess Di's mates and tea time and crumpets. Even the bloody "windy-pops," Nigel's classical euphemism for farts.

Jim stepped forward extending his hand, "Steve, how're you doing? Have you been waiting long?"

I shook his hand firmly, glad to see him, but not quite so glad to see Carol and the tall woman beside her with the funny hat. "No, Jim, I just got here. You're right on time."

Carol sidled up beside Jim. She was not exactly a pretty woman; she had rather squarish and masculine facial features along with very clear healthy skin and an athletic body. She was a very warmhearted person, with tremendous common sense and a very strong constitution. The most striking impression that she left was one of those people who always knew exactly what to do, in every situation. In her work, as the head nurse in the Oncology Department at the Children's Hospital, she had to be that way. I think that her day-to-day wisdom and ability to deal with life so simply, so clearly, was one of the things that riveted Jim to her so firmly. Jim needed balance, especially after the collapse of his affair with Nancy, the married woman, and Carol had come along and popped into Jim's life at exactly the right time to provide him with security. To this day, I still believe that Jim has become too dependent on Carol's strength; when I close my eyes and think of the two of them I can imagine Jim riding on Carol's back. Some thrive on Carol's strength, but I felt myself continually trying to escape from her good-willed embrace. This evening, and the woman with the funny hat and earring through her left nostril, would be part of that embrace, a hold that would prove slightly awkward to disentangle myself from.

Carol smiled and made the introduction, "Steve, this is Duffy McGraw. Duffy, meet Steve Miller. Or should I say Dr. Miller?"

I extended my hand somewhat uncomfortably, "Steve is fine,

thank you, Carol," I replied rather wistfully. Did I feel a slight pressure on my palm when we shook hands? It was hard to be sure since I had been looking at Carol, angry with her for the childish attempt to impress Duffy with my doctor title. Maybe it's a good thing I don't have tenure yet, I thought with a wince of guilt and pain all rolled together. In a few years she'll be introducing me as Professor Miller. That'll really push them away. I got further carried away and remembered what Hans, a German postdoc who once worked with me in Boston, had revealed about titles in Germany. The official title of a university researcher there is Herr Doctor Professor. Imagine that—Herr Doctor Professor Miller. If I were to pick up the phone and answer using that ridiculous title here in North America, there would be nobody left on the line by the time I got to my name.

I looked at Duffy, trying not to let her see that I was scrutinizing her. She was wearing a short, light ski-type jacket, in those fluorescent colors that are now so popular but won't be by next year. The jacket together with her heavy winter boots gave her the appearance of being much taller than she really was, but nevertheless she was still a few centimeters taller than I was. From what I could see until now, Duffy had the type of figure that was attractive to most males, including me. Tall, with nicely rounded hips, she had a shapely behind which I did not yet have the privilege of viewing or inspecting more closely. She also possessed rather firmly molded breasts. Yes, I could imagine that she turned a few heads when she walked down the street. I felt that her pretty face was partly disfigured by the earring running through her nose and that funny looking hat. But I was only a dull scientist with a conservative outlook. Nevertheless, I didn't think that she needed too much artificial help to catch attention.

We passed the potbellied, middle-aged, mustached ticket inspectors in their traditionally ugly red blazers and moved on to find our seats. Jim was a big hockey fan; he always had been. We used to skate together at the corner rink not far from Wascana Drive back in Regina, passing the puck back and forth and imagining the glory of Stanley Cup playoffs. I wasn't a bad skater and even now would lace on the blades for an occasional outing here in Toronto, but Jim was terrible. Skating up and down the ice with him I would feel much as my dog Compo must feel when accompanying me on nature hikes; since the pace is so slow for him, he whizzes back and forth probably accumulating an extra three kilometers for every one that I walk. That's the way it was skating with Jim. "Stick to tennis," I'd say to him, when he'd ask if I thought he was improving his skating technique. Perhaps that's why he maintained his fascination with professional hockey. Jim's architectural firm supported the Toronto Maple Leafs, buying four season tickets every year. They probably knocked that off their income tax anyway, and the partners took turns using the tickets. Even Jim wasn't fanatical enough to be interested in attending the entire forty home games that the Leafs played during the season.

Pushing our way through the crowds already equipped with their pregame beers and cigarettes, we finally passed through the correct gate and arrived at Jim's row. My mind began to toy with the intricate possibilities of the seating arrangements. I thought back to my high school mathematics teacher, Mr. Prokofyev, with his thick, square, black-framed glasses, who had taught us combinations and permutations so patiently. This particular calculation was a linear one; on the logical assumption that Carol and Jim would sit beside each other, that would leave a very limited number of possibilities. One of them was that Carol and Jim would sit together in the middle two seats, with me flanking Jim on one side and Duffy flanking Carol on the other. I desperately hoped that this order would materialize, because despite a slight panging sensation in me that anticipated some sort of interaction with Duffy, I did not feel up to the occasion emotionally. Another seating possibility was that the two men, Jim and myself, sit on the outskirts, with Duffy beside Carol and me, and Carol wedged in between Duffy and Jim. I did not look forward to this setup; I preferred to be away from Duffy and close to Jim. As it turned out, Carol smoothly took charge and made sure that Duffy and I were sitting beside each other, with Jim on the other side of me, and Duffy on the other side of her. I should have guessed that Carol, with her good-heartedness, would sacrifice sitting beside Jim in favor of allowing optimal conditions for the development of any channel of communications between Duffy and me, while ensuring that neither Duffy nor I were too uncomfortable. Trust Carol. Sometimes I could kick her. At the same time, glancing furtively at Duffy, I could not remain entirely indifferent to that nagging sensation that in a bolder mood I would definitely classify as lust.

Before the opening face-off Duffy still had a few minutes to get in some questions, and I replied politely, trying to volunteer as little additional information as possible. During my polite attempts to reciprocate with some partially feigned interest of my own, I learned that Duffy was also a nurse, in the Department of Ophthalmology at the hospital, and that she had met Carol some time ago on her lunch break in the hospital cafeteria. It seems that Carol had been planning this matchup for some time, because Duffy noted that Carol had mentioned me quite a while ago, on one of their first meetings at the hospital cafeteria. I could just picture Carol spooning up greasy potatoes and discussing poor Steve with Duffy. The images I conjured up did not particularly help make me feel more comfortable. I wondered whether the face-off between Duffy and me would be as interesting a match as the face-off between the Canadiens and the Leafs down on the ice. I also wondered whether it would remain as cool as the ice down below or heat up as these games often do.

The hockey game began punctually. I always preferred going to Leaf games against Montreal, Vancouver, or another Canadian team; it bugged the hell out of me to stand for so long and listen to two national anthems. Back in Regina, I could remember once when dad was feeling well and took Ervin and me to see the Regina Regents play the Russian Red Army team. Now *that* was a national anthem! We could see the hockey players begin to shift their weight from skate to skate in an attempt to loosen a few leg muscles. I think the Soviet anthem was longer than the first period of the game.

Jim quickly got into the action. He was one of those fans who becomes absorbed in the game, calling out jeers and catcalls to the referees whenever he was convinced that the Leafs had been given the short end of the stick. I noticed that Jim's behavior at the hockey games had deteriorated from the previous season, too. He was no longer just critical of the referees but was also obsessed with the efforts of his adopted Leafs. He would turn to me, or the man on his right, whom I presumed that he knew but later realized that he did not, and slur out comments like, "They just aren't skating tonight!" I wasn't surprised so much by the intensity of his comments and the degree of seriousness by which he took the game, but his sharp criticisms did seem somewhat unusual. After all, the Leafs were winning 3-0 at the end of the first period. Suddenly I realized that perhaps Carol wasn't making all that great a sacrifice by seating Duffy and me between Jim and herself.

At the end of the first period, Jim ordered us all beers and we chatted about the chances that the Leafs could make it to the Stanley Cup this year. I think that Carol, Duffy, and I couldn't really have cared less, but no one wanted to insult Jim, especially here at the Gardens. Throughout the game, over the cheers and applause of the crowd, Duffy tried to maintain some semblance of a conversation with me. I could tell that I would soon have a new problem on my hands. I actually *liked* Duffy; in spite of that earring running through her nose and her funny hat, she seemed a nice person, rather refreshing. I could also feel a moderate attraction to her, which further complicated matters, since I had no intention of getting involved with her. She was simply not my type, and I was not planning another disastrous relationship. I would not allow it this time.

When the game ended, with Toronto winning 6-2, Jim became his usual calm self again. Carol suggested that we all head for a bite to eat at Benito's, a popular Mexican food restaurant. I just wanted to get home, tired from a long day at work, but it was too early to make that plea without appearing rude, and everyone was really set for Mexican food. We plodded out of the Gardens, fighting our way through the cigarette smoke. It always amazed me how many smokers would attend these hockey games. After all, you'd think that these people would have some sort of empathy for the athletes, some connection to sports and fitness. However, it took me many years to learn to confine my rational thoughts to science; they just didn't fit in with the everyday world.

As we moved into the dark parking lot, Carol said, "Duffy, why don't you go with Steve in his car so he won't be all alone and we'll meet at the restaurant. If you get there first, grab a non-smoking table."

So I walked on with Duffy in the cold night to my car, wedged firmly in a traffic jam in the very position where it had been parked a few hours earlier. Duffy tried to ask questions about my work, where I lived, and what my hobbies were. I made every effort to be polite and patient, but tried my best to come out as a very boring, ordinary "bloke," as old Nigel would say. I wanted her to come to her own conclusions regarding me. I tried very hard to swing the conversation to her work and activities. When she mentioned her passion for skiing, I quickly noted, "You won't catch me on those things, I'm too much of a chicken for that." I wanted to make her feel that I was too conservative for her, too "old" emotionally, if not by age itself. I must have been seven or eight years older anyway. However, nothing I said seemed to put Duffy off, or else she too was being terribly polite. Even worse, I had the feeling that she had slid her hand over near the gear shift so that each time I maneuvered into fourth gear, there would be light contact. I opened my window slightly for some cool air and tried to remain in third gear as long as possible.

Although it seemed to me an eternity, valiantly striving to remain unaffected by Duffy in the short drive to Benito's, we arrived fairly quickly. Jim and Carol were already inside with a table waiting. That didn't surprise me, because although Jim was not a speedster, I had been driving most of the way in third gear. We sat down opposite each other, and although I noticed that Duffy had removed her silly hat and that her cheeks were rosy red from the short hike from the parking lot, I did not realize that she was without her ski jacket. We had all hung our coats over the backs of our chairs, all of course except for Duffy.

Jim took charge with the menu, ordering tacos and tortillas and a number of other Mexican treats for us to all share. He resorted to his standard Mexican restaurant joke (this was a common place to come for a snack on the way home after watching a hockey game with Jim), saying, "This Mexican restaurant has great food—just don't drink the water." I noticed Carol staring off at the lights when he said this, but Duffy laughed amiably. I supposed that this might be funny the first time you hear it, but that was so long ago I could no longer remember if I had thought this was funny at the time or not. Probably not, I thought nastily, if Duffy was laughing at it now.

It seemed as though the roles reversed after Jim finished ordering and Carol took control of the conversation. She seemed intent on hunting for areas of joint interest between Duffy and me, and anything would do. When Duffy mentioned that she had been in Switzerland last Christmas skiing, Carol immediately told her that I had been in South America doing some hiking in the Andes. Andes, Alps, hiking, skiing, South America, Europe—for Carol these were minor differences that showed how common our interests were. I don't even think Duffy felt entirely comfortable by these overly blatant little tricks that Carol was trying. Yet despite all this, Duffy would flash me a pretty, knowing smile now and then, when she thought that Carol wasn't looking. I could also feel some pressure on my leg under the table that could not be attributed to Duffy simply stretching her long legs.

As the evening began to wind down, with Jim pouncing on the bill, claiming that the evening was "his treat" (Jim was always very generous, especially now that he could really afford to be), Carol tried to formulate a sequel. I politely deferred any attempts for a four-way meeting, claiming that my schedule was in my office and that I didn't remember what arrangements I had made offhand. I could sense that Carol felt badly that her proposed matchup might not succeed. I promised her that I would check my schedule and be in contact within the next few days. I began to feel as though the danger was dissipating, and a certain relief, albeit mingled with the disappointment at missing a potentially exciting encounter, flooded and confused my emotions. When we exited the restaurant, Jim said thoughtfully, "I think it'll be easier if we drop you off at home, Duffy. Your place is a little out of the way for Steve."

"Sure, thanks, Jim," said Duffy. "Oh, but my jacket is in Steve's car."

The ball was now firmly in my court. Not only was the ball in my court, but upon retrieving it, I was going to have to make a split-second decision whether to attempt a defensive lob or try to pass my opponent with force at the net. I now realized that I had not imagined any of Duffy's light touches. Before me lay several possibilities, but I had very little time to consider them. I could simply jog to the car and bring Duffy her jacket. My rational, scientific side was pushing me to do that. However, a strong co-alition devised of loneliness, sexual urges, ego, and various other unidentifiable feelings was acting upon me. "That's all right, Jim. I'll take Duffy home. It's not that far out of the way, especially at this time of the night. There's no traffic," I explained. Here was the attempt to rationalize those feelings again. When would I learn that the world wasn't composed mainly of science and scientists, I thought wistfully.

Duffy gladly accepted my offer and we bid our mutual friends good night. I supposed that Carol must have been relieved by now. As we drove along the almost deserted Toronto avenues, Duffy was telling me how much she enjoyed the evening and how accurately Carol had described me. I carried on with her conversation, but was immersed in calculations of where this was leading. I knew now that I could simply take Duffy home, and that would be that. If she were hurt, that would be her problem; I didn't ask her to leave her jacket in my car. If I did take Duffy straight home to her apartment, the ball would then again be in her court, because she might or might not invite me up to her place. Making swift calculations, I decided that I did not want to decide anything; I would take her home and see how things progressed. When we finally stopped in front of her building, she reached over and switched off my headlights—the car's headlights that is. Before I could even think clearly she was kissing me firmly and had her arm around me and her hand dwindling under my jacket, pushing its way under my sweater and shirt. "Would you like to come up with me?" she whispered into my ear.

I pulled back a little and said, "You know, Duffy, I am quite attracted to you. I'm just not into the phase where I can handle a relationship right now—"

She cut me off quickly, "Steve, don't speak to me like a child. I'm not a little virgin girl living with mommy and daddy. Who said anything about a relationship? All I asked was whether you'd like to come up to my apartment with me—right now. I won't be insulted if you decline, but I deserve an answer which isn't condescending."

I looked at her oddly, as if she had astonished me. I felt foolish; she certainly had caught me by surprise. I switched off the ignition and we headed up to her apartment, arm in arm.

CHAPTER FIVE

From the corner of the corridor near my office, I could see that the doors belonging to my lab were open; it was likely that Opera-Singh, Neal, or both had arrived as they were early birds. I unlocked my own office and decided to pull myself together before checking up on them. I closed the door, and pulled down the shade that covered the window on the inside of the door. I did not feel interested in any uninvited visitors. My answering machine had about five messages, all of which I guessed were from yesterday evening. It was now only 7:45 a.m. and very few people were likely to call my office before nine. I turned down the volume of my answering machine and played back the messages quietly. There was one message to call the secretary from the institute, two messages from other scientists in the institute, and two messages, both the first and last, from my ex-wife Jeannie. Please call as soon as possible, it's important, was their content. I thought again of poor Compo and having to give him up for another few months. On the other hand, Compo didn't have an easy life, even with me. After all, even last night I arrived home at four in the morning with the poor dog waiting for me to take him out. He had sniffed me all over when I arrived home, as if to say "I know who you were with and what you were doing." That dog could be so bloody human, almost judgmental sometimes.

That thought suddenly disturbed me. Was I not judgmental myself? Had I not prejudged Duffy and mistaken her intentions? Apparently. I had a great time with her last night, rolling around on her queen sized bed—pure sex, with no strings attached. It often escaped me that women, too, had physical yearnings of their own. Although I considered myself to be extremely liberal, and a strong supporter of feminism, some things are still woven too firmly into my consciousness. I had always believed that something in the physiological makeup of men induced a distinct type of libido from that felt by women. With women, I was of the conviction that lust must be accompanied by emotional feelings, otherwise it fizzles out. Meanwhile, it is common knowledge that men easily separate lust from love. Now I learned that some women also discern between these feelings and experience them apart from each other. Perhaps my presumptuous conclusions—that women generally are unable to relate to love and lust independently—may be due to conditioning pushed on women by our still male-dominated society.

Despite feeling a jump in my self-esteem from my encounter with Duffy, I was beginning to feel pangs of guilt regarding my association with Julia Kearns. I kept justifying my behavior by reasoning with myself that my sexual adventures with Duffy would not interfere with anything connected to Julia. Nevertheless, I could not be entirely convinced. There was still a nagging feeling that I had done something wrong.

I collected my thoughts together, planned my day, and set out to see who was there in the lab. Opera-Singh hadn't arrived yet, but Neal was there with timers beeping and his hands flying out everywhere, marking tubes and pushing buttons on the various pieces of equipment in the lab.

"Good morning, Neal," I said. "What's up?"

"Morning, Steve," he answered still pushing buttons and turning knobs. "By the way, did you hear about the new drug for Alzheimer's?"

It was the second time that month that he played that foolery on me, but I fell for it again. "No, Neal, what drug?"

He looked at me with glassy eyes, "Drug? What drug? Are you taking drugs?"

I was stupid enough to forge on, "The one you just said they developed for Alzheimer's disease!"

"For who?" he said stonily, starting to drive me crazy, "What are you on about?" Neal enjoyed winding me up now and then, and I was too careless to avoid his little traps.

He realized the joke was over and said casually, "I've got some interesting results to show you later."

"Great," I replied. "I'll let you get on with your work. Come see me when you have some time later." The truth is that Neal was starting to make me feel dizzy. He had that effect of perpetual motion, as though the world was about to end, and he was furiously racing to finish up before that. I thought back and found it hard to believe that I, too, had once worked like that. Well, perhaps not quite so intensely, but with the same resoluteness. Things for me were now so slow, so calm. I did not look back with envy at those days where I carried out my own experiments, during my doctoral studies here in Toronto, or in the midst of my postdoctoral research in Boston. It's true that there was always more excitement on the bench than at the computer terminal. The suspense and adrenaline of executing a complex experiment and anxiously awaiting the results was a prime motivator for many young researchers, but I now enjoyed the academic side of the work: strategic planning of what we should be studying, proposing new experiments in the grant applications, interpreting and discussing results with my students and Opera-Singh, and polishing the writing of our articles. I know that many of my colleagues in similar principal investigator positions really miss the good old days of actual experimentation; they are bored of the writing and teaching and would love to go back to the bench and do the work themselves. I don't. Perhaps one day that will change. Then again, I highly doubt it.

Neal looked up at me suddenly, "Oh, by the way, Jeannie called yesterday and asked me to tell you that she wants you to call her. Twice."

Neal knew who Jeannie was and although we never spoke of my marriage, he showed additional sensitivity here. If it had been anyone else, he would have been complaining how he had been disturbed in the lab. He was especially incensed with the people who first called my office and, not wanting to leave a message on my answering machine, tried again at the lab. Many times I would walk into the lab and hear Neal say into the phone, "Leave a message on his machine, he'll be more likely to get it. I'm his student, not his secretary." He had a point there. However, with Jeannie, Neal was especially restrained, as though he could somehow make things better between us by being nice. To me it was almost touching; I knew Neal quite well.

"Thanks, Neal, I'll call her back before she calls here again. I hope she didn't take up too much of your time."

Neal waved me off with a gesture, and I decided that I had better try calling Jeannie. It was still early, but she had said this was urgent. I settled down again in my padded office chair and called, preparing myself emotionally for those uncommunicative conversations. We were both bad at talking on the phone, and this condition had only regressed since we separated a few years ago. To be fair, we had been bad at communication not just over the phone, but via any media, including the most direct one, face to face. However, as her phone line rang, I particularly remembered the numerous, stunted, awkward attempts to remain in contact by phone over the past three years, with long, heavy, oppressive silences on the other end of the telephone line. My British mate, Nigel, who had fostered a particular dislike of Jeannie, would once say that he "had just had a nice monologue with her," after bumping into her in Eaton's downtown store.

"Hello?" I heard a sleepy voice. Oh shit, I thought, not only is it hard to talk to her, but I just woke her up. But my confidence returned quickly. "Hello, Jeannie?"

"Just a minute," Jeannie replied. "I'll be right back." I waited realizing that it's often more or less the same silence at the other end of the line whether she's there or not, but she soon returned.

"Jeannie," I said, "sorry to wake you but I was a little worried receiving all those messages from you. Is something wrong?"

"No, nothing's wrong, but I need to speak to you right away," she answered.

I thought to myself, this doesn't sound exactly like she's only missing the dog, but I waited for her to go on. "I'm listening," I said.

"No, not now, not here on the phone," she said in that familiar exasperated tone. I was glad that she was on the other end of the line and not here beside me. "Are you free for dinner tonight?"

"Tonight?" I reiterated with surprise; I had hoped to recover from my sleepless night with Duffy.

"Yes, tonight. I need to see you right away."

"Alright," I said, "just not at Benito's. I can't handle Mexican food again." I knew that she wouldn't see the humor in this, but I said it anyway. Even if she had understood the reason why I had said this, I knew that she still wouldn't have seen the humor in it.

The day wore on with the usual events. I jumped every time the phone rang, afraid that it would either be Julia or Duffy, not wanting it to be either of them. But neither of them called. Julia probably had no idea whatsoever that I had any nonscientific interest in her, and Duffy made it clear that last night was an exceptional and one-time event for her too. For some strange reason, I felt hurt. Although I clearly did not want to begin a relationship with Duffy, my ego was nonetheless insulted to find that she, too, was not interested in continuing to see me. Suddenly I felt tremendous empathy with all those women who complained that they had been "stood up" by men after one-night stands. In this case, like Duffy, I was just as resolved to contain the situation to a single night. I imagined how hurt and disgruntled I would have felt had I actually hoped and intended for things to develop beyond a one-night stand.

Neal came to discuss his results. Things were shaping up well; Neal had developed a system that allowed him to see biochemical changes in both nerve and blood cells from animals with a certain form of depression that the scientific community generally agreed was similar to a human depressive disorder. We scientists called this a "model system." I was already weighing the possibility of adapting Neal's system to our expanding study, the proposed research with Julia on the bipolar disorder patients. Neal was going to be a good scientist, and his work on this new animal model, if it could be verified by diligent and cautious repetition along with the addition of many more "controls"—healthy "non-depressed" animals—(to ensure that the results were truly meaningful) would definitely merit publishing in another prestigious journal. It might even eventually lead to the development of some new pharmaceutical tools, but that was a long way away. Basic research is always a long way from the clinical trials; our fundamental studies may be at the forefront of research, but they are often long forgotten by the time the drugs are developed. I encouraged Neal, trying not to inflate his ego any more, and sent him off to repeat his experiments.

Opera-Singh also came in the afternoon to discuss some of his results. He was having trouble calibrating a certain line of experimentation and was even more peevish than usual. "It is being very difficult to find answer," Opera-Singh complained. "Maybe we are trying to buy commercial kit for assay." What Opera-Singh wanted was to save some hassle by actually buying a ready-made kit that would allow experimentation without all the painful calibration stages. I agreed with him that the kit would certainly be faster, but reminded him that we were not yet a rich lab and at present we simply could not afford to buy kits for everything. I reassured him that if the line of experimentation didn't work out, we would buy a kit the following week.

"But Neal is saying that you are receiving several new grants," he insisted. "There not being money for kit this week?"

"Come on, Singh," I said, "don't give up. If we solve the problem without the kit, we'll be much freer to do the studies. I promise that we'll buy it if you don't succeed by the end of this week."

"Alright," he shrugged, "but I not take the blame if experiment is not working."

I invested my free time, despite my weariness, on my grant application and managed to progress reasonably well. I calculated that another two or three days of full concentration, either at home on the weekend or early next week, would suffice to allow me to present Julia with a decently written first draft. I worked even more conscientiously than usual, aware that I hoped to impress Julia with the quality of the application.

The end of the workday came quickly. I spoke to Tania, who was still absorbing techniques from Neal. I think that she, too, resorted to swallowing aspirins at the end of the day to get over the dizziness Neal invoked. Ken also came in to consult me regarding his courses for the second semester, which was still several months away. He made the impression of a very serious, persevering student, who liked to be organized well in advance. I appreciated that and tried to direct him to the courses that I believed would be most beneficial to him. I left the lab somewhat early, around five, requesting as usual that Neal lock up properly. As I left the lab, I could hear him say to Tania, "The day he forgets to tell me to lock up properly, we'll know he's starting to go senile."

Back home Compo was surprised to see me so early. In fact, I caught him curled up like a ball, his elongated head taking advantage of my pillow on the bed in my bedroom. I try to remember to shut the door to my room so that he doesn't do that. He's allowed on the sofa in the living room, but I try to stop him from climbing all over me in my bed. When I lived with Jeannie, he used to sleep with us on the bed at night. I would usually wake up in the wee hours of the winter mornings, feeling mild frostbite developing in my toes and find Compo snoring away, lying between us with his head pushed under the quilt. Compo is all that's left between us now, I thought. He may have been all that we had in common for some time before we separated.

71

I wrestled him off the bed, determined again not to leave the bedroom door open. Compo was a great actor. He got off the bed with his tail between his legs, rolled onto the floor and lay on his back with his paws in the air, as if to say, "Do what you want with me. I'm at your mercy." But he was also tremendously stubborn, and if I were to leave the door open again, the entire situation would simply recur like a lesson in déjà vu.

After taking Compo out for a "double" as Jeannie used to say, I showered and dressed to meet her for dinner. I was tired, and glad that it was already Thursday. Although I planned to take a lot of work home for the weekend, I still looked forward to the change. The idea of working at home, and not in my office at the institute, appealed to me. I also looked forward to tennis with Jim at the club and even to a home-cooked meal with Mom and Paul tomorrow evening. But first I must get through this evening. This was an extremely unusual situation; my relationship with Jeannie since our separation and divorce, although civil, had been managed almost exclusively by phone. Only those meetings somewhere between our flats on some Toronto street to shuttle Compo back and forth had given either of us a chance to see one another over the past three years. We had not met anywhere else. And now, out of the blue, I receive an urgent invitation to dinner from her. I did not fool myself, though. There had been an irritable edge in her voice on the phone this morning; whatever it was that she wanted, it couldn't be good.

We met at the entrance to Raymond's, which had once been a favorite of ours. We found a nonsmoking table and sat down opposite each other. I could tell that Jeannie was tense. One didn't need to be a psychologist to see that she was under some kind of stress and that something was bothering her.

"Wine, Jeannie?" I asked.

"What?" she wasn't paying attention. "No, thanks, not tonight."

We made small talk until the waitress had taken our orders and gone off to another table. I always hated having people listen in to my private conversations, even if they couldn't have cared less about whatever it was that I was talking about. I looked at Jeannie sitting rather stiffly across from me. She was a thin woman of about thirty-five, and she looked exactly her age, no more, no less. She had red hair and freckles, with pleasant features. She was dressed a little too formally for me; I had been used to seeing her in jeans and T-shirts, but I guess that many people change their taste in clothing as they go through life. I certainly hadn't.

Jeannie worked at the largest sewage plant in Toronto. Although she was the manager of human resources and was not involved with the chemical processes carried out by the plant, I did get a certain satisfaction in telling Jim and other acquaintances that my ex-wife runs a sewage plant. Indeed, my former mother-in-law (with whom I was still on good terms) used to say that Jeannie received benefits that included "stink pay."

I leaned towards her and asked, "What's up?" Apparently she had been waiting for this.

"I have something to tell you," she said quietly.

I was too weary for her riddles now. "I know you do, you mentioned that this morning," I answered with a trace of sarcasm, knowing it was wasted on her.

She gathered herself together, literally, first rubbing her hair, and then her hands together as if trying to dry them with one of those horrid restaurant washroom hand dryers. There's probably one in the men's room here, I thought to myself stupidly. "Steve, I'm getting married," she finally uttered.

"Good for you," I replied almost mechanically. I really didn't know what else to say. In fact, I didn't quite understand why she couldn't have used the phone, which was our usual channel for whatever semblance of communication we had between us in recent years.

"I'm getting married to Martin early next week," she continued, as though I hadn't heard her first announcement.

"Luvlee," I found myself borrowing another one from Nigel. I wondered whether he also used my own patented Canadian phrases and expressions when he went back to London to visit his friends and family. Again, I didn't know what else to say. If this had been a phone call, we probably would each have thought that the line had gone dead.

I took a sip of my beer and thought of Jeannie and Martin. I couldn't stand Martin. I had formed a strong dislike of him right from the start, years before he had begun to court Jeannie in spite of our marriage. Although by now I had lost my view of the sanctity and significance of marriage, at the time I had taken Jeannie's affair with Martin rather poorly. I had even once threatened "to kick the shit out of him," but I had never actually acted on that impulse. I no longer cared about the affair or about our divorce. Still, I wanted no connection with that good-for-nothing layabout. Martin had inherited a chain of nationwide food stores. He was lazy and made little effort to contribute to the still-expanding family business. Contrary to Jeannie's claims, I was not jealous of his wealth or so-called freedom. Many times I had told her that had I wanted to be wealthy, I would have chosen business administration or law rather than science. I was always put off that she, who was supposed to understand me, could not grasp that I never had ambitions of being wealthy. No, I simply could not stand his pompousness; especially since he had precious little reason to be pompous aside from family money.

Jeannie looked at me again and said, "That's not all, either."

I took another sip of my beer and said with a mildly sarcastic tone, "You mean you're marrying someone else, too?"

"Don't be ridiculous," she said dryly. She had never learned to appreciate my cynical humor while we were married, and I didn't expect her to appreciate my snide remarks now. Good thing she doesn't work with Neal, I chuckled to myself.

"Martin must move to Seattle for business reasons, and I'm going with him."

"I hear Seattle is a pretty city," was all I could think of saying.

Then she broke down. Until then I hadn't really fully grasped the problem. She wanted my blessing. Jeannie knew exactly what

I thought of Martin. The two of them had now been living together since our separation and to some degree even before that. She knew that I would wish her well, and that I wanted her to be happy. This much was true. But she had been hoping that I would forgive Martin. She believed that my hatred of Martin stemmed from his taking her away from me. How naïve! How egocentric! If Martin hadn't started his affair with Jeannie, I knew that someone else would have. I knew that our marriage had been doomed the instant it arrived at the point where either of us would even contemplate an affair. I despised Martin independently of his involvement with Jeannie, long before he displayed any romantic interest in her. The way he took advantage of people, his general laziness, and his low caliber personality disgusted me. Obviously his affair with Jeannie while we were still married hadn't exactly improved my opinion of him. But Jeannie didn't understand this. She was convinced of my personal vendetta against "poor Martin." So be it. There was only so much I could take. And I had lost my will to explain things to her.

"Steve," she said, her voice quivering in a beggar's tone, "would you please give Martin a call and wish him the best? It would mean so much to him. He still feels badly about what's happened."

I looked at her, still struggling to understand. "Listen, Jeannie, I wish you the best, and that you be happy with *him* (I even hated using his name), but no, I will not speak to him. I have nothing to say to him and want nothing to do with him. He doesn't deserve my attentions and I have no intention of giving them to him."

"You are so obstinate," she declared.

"What do you care?" I retorted angrily. "You are out of my obstinate clutches now. You're free of me, but you act as though we are Siamese twins."

Jeannie calmed down a little and the tension eased once her expectations of me had plummeted. We managed to get through dinner and even have a few laughs about old times. I was exhausted, both emotionally and physically by the end of the meal, and after a quick cup of café-au-lait, we said our good-byes and promised to keep in touch occasionally by e-mail.

When I finally sat down and turned the ignition in my car, a sudden thought dawned on me. I was immediately ecstatic. Compo could not go with them to Seattle; he was here to stay with me for a long time in Toronto. That is, of course, if I ever receive my tenure here I thought to myself bitterly, as guilt and worry overrode my short-lived ecstasy.

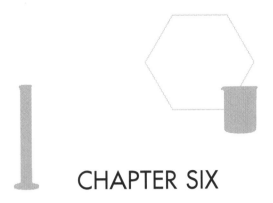

CHAPTER SIX

"I love Fridays," grinned Neal as I walked into the lab. "It's nice and quiet, the phones aren't ringing away, and I can finally get some work done."

I glanced around the lab, and compared with the usual whirlwind of activity and the constant hum and buzz of people prancing in the corridors, it did seem suddenly a rather pastoral atmosphere. When I wanted to concentrate on work in my office on Fridays, I didn't usually need to disconnect the phone.

"Did you see my latest attempt to keep the phone from slowing down my work?" Neal quizzed me.

"No," I answered. I peeked over to look around the corner of the lab and ensure that the phone was still there, immediately suspicious that Neal had tossed the thing out the sixth story window.

Reading my thoughts, Neal replied, "No, I didn't chuck it out the window. I use it too, you know." He whisked over to the table and picked up the phone; I could now see what he had changed. He held a cordless phone in his hand. "Look," he grinned widely, like a child with a chocolate bar all to himself, "I can walk all the way around the department and make orders on the phone while getting ice from the ice machine or even while I'm in the department library." He leaned towards me with an even more ludicrous grin, "I can even handle university bureaucracy on the phone *while taking a crap*. Now isn't that fitting! Or should I say 'fitting shitting'?!"

I laughed heartily and agreed with Neal that it certainly was fitting, and I praised his innovative spirit. But I had come to speak to Neal for a good reason. "Neal, I have a proposition for you."

"I'm listening, boss."

"Do you remember Jack McMann?" I asked him. Neal had a great memory for names. In fact, he was often complaining and spouting his theory that these excessive names trapped in his memory were taking up valuable space. "I've only got so much room up here," he would say tapping his forehead. "Every additional name I remember makes me forget someone's birthday, a high school trigonometry formula, a phone number, or something else that's important."

He remembered McMann. "Yeah, that's the guy who wrote all those papers on the genetic studies dealing with schizophrenia."

"Right," I said, "that's the same McMann."

"Well, what about him? He hasn't decided to start moving in on our project, has he?" Neal was always on the verge of paranoia, afraid that some big American research group would push their way into our field and angle us out. We both knew that this could happen: a larger research group could push ahead into our niche and publish their own results before we could publish ours. Fat chance of that, I supposed, with Neal on this project. His prolific work style and output was probably on par with three to four normal researchers. Obviously I didn't say that to him.

"No, Neal, he hasn't begun to compete with us. Your paranoia is something we should try studying in the lab. Would you volunteer to give a blood sample? McMann is a senior editor of a new journal that publishes review articles in our field."

"What's it called," Neal jeered slightly, "*Down and Out* or *Deep Depression*?"

"It's called *Annual Review of Depressive Disorders*. McMann sent me an e-mail and asked if I'd like to contribute a review on our field of study." This was clearly an honor, albeit a small one (the journal was clearly not the most prestigious in the field, but it was considered to be a decent scientific journal). Moreover, a review was different from writing up a regular article. It meant that I was considered to be a relative expert in my field, and that itself was no small feat for a tenure-seeking young (or not-so-young) faculty member. In fact, it might well prove to be a small bonus that will help me pad my curriculum vitae and publication list in favor of that ever-elusive tenure. Neal, too, despite his brash outward manner, was impressed. I said to him, "Neal, would you like to write the article with me?"

I thought that his eyes would bulge out of his head at first, but Neal regained his calm relatively quickly. "Sure, why not? When's the deadline? How long is it supposed to be?" Neal had already grasped the idea and was trying to calculate the practical aspects of the deal.

"I'll send my approval, and then ask McMann for the details. Our departmental library doesn't stock the journal, and I'd prefer looking at an entire volume rather than printing out only a few online papers. So, when you have a few minutes, pop down to the main library and bring us a sample of the journal so we can see what the papers in it are like. I'm acquainted with the journal, but not all that well."

Neal practically burst, "A few minutes to pop down to the library? Man, are you out of it!"

"Well, how long does it take to pick up a journal from the main library downstairs?" I asked innocently, falling into his neat little trap.

"With the elevators out again, quite some time," he answered offhandedly.

"Are they out again? The bastards—"

"Now you're talking," encouraged Neal, pleased with himself. "That's the spirit."

Before finally amassing and packing all my work to take home for the weekend, Neal came by the lab and thanked me for the opportunity to include him in the writing of the review paper. It's true, it is quite an honor for a Ph.D. student to write a scientific review paper, but Neal did deserve it. But that's not what I told him.

"You'll have even more work to do, now, Neal. Let's hope you can manage to put together a decent review. We'll discuss this next week. Have a good weekend."

"Weekend?" he snorted. "I'll be here today until late, and again on both Saturday and Sunday. Some weekend!"

"I thought that you'd at least stop complaining for once with the review ahead of you," I chided him. That worked; Neal smiled that peculiar sarcastic smile that was his hallmark and charged back to the lab, to his quiet domain and newly acquired cordless phone.

At home, later in the afternoon, I asked Compo the classical million-dollar question, "Want to come with me to Mom and Paul's?" His answer was first characterized by leaping at least fifteen centimeters in the air off his hind legs. Even Michael Jordan wouldn't be ashamed of a vertical like that. However, just like the routine when I came home from the supermarket, there was a necessity to shift my body ninety degrees to be at right angles with Compo in order not to get the wind knocked out of me. Upon landing, Compo would go crazy bouncing around, sneezing with excitement and even emit the odd "Ouuuuaaa" that was an even more advanced way of expressing his excitement. I took the liberty of interpreting his combined responses as an affirmative reply to my original query. I bundled him down to my car and we drove, with Compo next to me in the front seat, out to Mom and Paul's little house. He was well behaved in the car and only licked my hand at red lights when the car was standing still. At least he didn't try any funny stuff when I shifted gears, as thoughts of Duffy and a sense of guilt washed over me again.

When we pulled up in front of the house, Compo was already all wound up. He knew just where we were and who we were about to visit. He loved Mom and especially Paul, but most of all, he loved the freedom, which included rampaging all over their little yard together with their little ginger-colored female cocker spaniel, Chupa. No sooner had I opened his car door than he was already pouncing on the front door of the house, his tail flagging away like a metronome. He greeted Mom and Paul with tremendous enthusiasm and hastily went to play with his dog friend in the yard out back. I locked the car doors and headed on into the house.

"Come on in, Steve. How're things going?" queried Paul as he took my coat and hung it neatly in the front hall closet.

Paul was a tall man of about sixty-five. His wide, big-boned, rugged, but clean-shaven face was matched with a straight, pug-like nose. He was the type of person who constantly emitted a consistent, logical, no-nonsense approach to whatever he undertook. Curiosity, politeness, respectfulness, and understanding formed the backbone of his character. Paul approved of things that were clear and simple, and he disliked intricate, disorganized affairs. For example, he hated politics. I liked Paul very much. He was a senior orthopedic surgeon at the Toronto Hospital for Sick Children, and I had even sent Neal to him once back when he had been limping around the lab for several days suffering from some knee problems. Most importantly, Paul had a wonderful effect on mom. He was good for her—very stable, very calm, very secure. He worshipped her and had wholeheartedly adopted our entire family. Although I looked to him as an older friend who was sincerely concerned with my best interests, I knew that Paul served as a father figure to both Cindy and Ervin.

"Steve, have you put on some weight?" Mom always tried to use those motherly clichés and act "like a mother," but these attempts were so transparent and artificial, that I think even Paul felt uncomfortable.

"Uh, no, I think it's just this sweater, mom." My weight hadn't changed since I was fifteen.

"Oh, I had been hoping that maybe you were going out with someone nice who might improve your dietary habits," complained mom, trying valiantly to act disappointed.

"Sorry to disappoint you, but I haven't been out with any

women for some time, mom. I've been extremely busy," I lied through my teeth thinking of Duffy.

Although I abhorred lies and dishonesty, in this case I felt that the end justified the means. I was determined not to leave any opening for conversation with mom about private affairs, especially my recent ones with Duffy. These were topics of conversation that I wouldn't even broach alone with Paul.

Mom was about the same age as Paul, with short grayish hair. She looked very trim and healthy; they both did. They spent several hours a day exercising on their treadmills, rowing machines, toning machines, and all those fancy contraptions. They had timers, skipping ropes, a universal, barbell sets, chalk for their handgrips, matching cotton towels, and a dedicated stereo system all set up for exercising. I recalled once having told Neal how their basement looked like a weight lifter's training room. They had so many different types of exercise apparatuses that I often wondered how they could possibly choose what type of workout to do each day. Neal pondered, "Maybe they have an extra centrifuge or something we could use here in the lab?" He never gave up that one-track line of thought.

Paul poured us each a beer and brought mom a glass of white wine, and we sat down in their comfortable little living room. The room was airy and sporty looking with a bright carpet and ample light. I thought that I would be lucky to have a place like this in twenty years' time. I would be luckier still to find a partner who could stand to live with me by then.

Paul had always been extremely interested in my work. Although his expertise lay in bone structure, he had the curiosity of a research scientist. I did not go into unnecessary details regarding my work, but Paul was able to grasp the general idea. This evening he began asking more about the practical and political aspects of my work.

"So, how long do you think they'll take to let you know about your tenure?" he asked earnestly.

"I really don't know. Three months ago, I thought that it would be any day. As time goes on, I realize that they don't seem to be in a hurry. Maybe they enjoy torturing me with the suspense."

Mom forced herself to concentrate on the conversation. "Who decides about your tenure?"

"It's a combination, mom. The institute ultimately decides, but they've sent my file away to a number of experts in my field to ask their opinion whether I'm worthy or not."

"What's the main criterion for the choice," Paul pressed, "or is it all politics like in the hospital?"

"I'd say that the main criterion is probably my publication list. After all, the only real way to assess the success of my research is by counting publications, and also considering in which journals the publications appear. For example, some journals are so prestigious, that one publication there is worth several publications in a more ordinary journal."

"Well, you've got lots of publications," said mom supportively. "How much more can they expect?"

"Yes, I have a reasonable number of publications, but the majority of them are still from my postdoctoral specialization period in Boston. The important publications for my tenure are my recent ones, where I am the senior author, the one who directs the research. The institute knows that I can carry out my own research already. That's what my Ph.D. and postdoctoral studies are supposed to illustrate. Tenure means they trust me to direct it, too, with my own students executing the work."

"What about that prize you received for teaching that course last year? That must be worth something, no?" Paul remembered everything.

"Yes, well, that certainly won't hurt my chances. Look, I'm cautiously optimistic that things will go through. It's just that there's so much tension while waiting for the answer. If it hadn't been so long since I applied, I wouldn't have this nagging apprehension. At any rate, if I'm not accepted, I have reason to believe that other universities might be interested in taking me. But I like Toronto." There was no point in being pessimistic with them and telling them how Bruce had lost his position.

We sat down for mom's Friday evening chicken dinner. Mom filled me in on family matters. Over the years I had lost contact with many of our relations back in Regina. "Ervin is looking for a job, again."

I looked aghast, "He didn't get fired, did he?" Ervin was a certified gym teacher, or rather physical education teacher as it was now called, but he had been bouncing around from school to school on the east coast in New Brunswick, Nova Scotia, and Prince Edward Island for several years. I recalled the famous cartoonist, Charles Schultz, once depicting in his *Charlie Brown* comic strip that, "Those who cannot do, teach. And those who cannot teach, teach gym."

Paul answered with a fatherly look, "No, Steve, he's still in New Brunswick at the same school, but he wants to try coaching semiprofessional hockey."

At first, I almost swallowed a chicken bone, but then I realized that Ervin's plan did not surprise me. Mom asked me, "Does he ever write to you?"

"Not really," I replied evasively.

"What do you mean 'not really'? For a scientist who should be exact, you can really be quite vague when you choose to be," mom noted.

"Well, I do get the odd note from him by e-mail," I answered unwillingly.

"What does he say? Why don't you tell me? And here I am thinking that there's no communication between you all these years."

"It's just that his messages are not really very informative. They are more like a certain type of greeting."

"That's fine," mom said optimistically. "The main thing is that he stays in contact with you. You know that deep down he respects you very much. Now how does he greet you in these messages?"

Not having much choice in the matter, I felt compelled to answer, "Well, at the beginning of the week, I opened my e-mail to find 643 messages from Ervin all saying the same thing: Fuck the Good Lord, Fuck Roy Winston."

Paul looked amused. He did not shock easily. Having treated so many car accident victims he was very tough emotionally, almost immune. I knew also that mom had filled him in on our entire childhood, our nightmare with Telia Mastpole, and some of the other traumatic childhood events.

Paul said, "Well, I knew Ervin was never really the religious type. I suppose that old bastard Preacher Winston can have that effect on anyone."

Mom, too, seemed less upset than I would have expected. "Keep trying to get through to him, Steve. He's lonely. He spends hours on the Internet. It's practically impossible to call him these days. He's also broken up with his latest girlfriend. It can't be easy for him."

"That seems a family trait," I remarked remorsefully.

"Let's hope not," Paul joked, and took mom's hand across the table. "I don't really think that's true. It's not easy to find someone to love and live with in today's world. The random chances of meeting someone who is perfect are really slim. I've been extremely lucky," Paul admitted, as though mom weren't even there.

Yes, I thought to myself, you've both been extremely fortunate with the way things have worked out. My mind wandered back twenty odd years to the circumstances that eventually led to their union.

CHAPTER SEVEN

The winter that I turned fourteen was a cold one, even by the rigorous standards of Saskatchewan. Even the town elderly complained that they hadn't had a winter like that in many years. The first snowfalls were already accumulating by mid-October, and the temperatures dropped to minus fifteen degrees Celsius. By November, the snow was piled high on the corners of all the side streets, but that never bothered us. It was the icy wind whistling through our hooded parkas that took its toll. The so-called windchill factor was so severe that in the mornings while waiting for the bus to school, we used to spit up in the air to see if the spittle would freeze before hitting the ground. Bryan Cooper, a neighbor who went to the same school as me, got bored of "horking" up into the air. He decided to try something original and to see how fast his urine would freeze. That was a bad mistake; he got his little willy caught on his frozen zipper and had to be taken to the hospital. The guys at school wouldn't leave him alone for the next four years, continually chiding him that the trauma would interfere with his future sex life.

Aside from the bitter cold that we all felt on the way to and from school, the exceptionally extreme winter was an additional burden on Ervin and myself. We liked to be out of the house as much as possible. Every hour spent away from home was a bonus for each of us. This was especially so on the frequent occasions when mom was away at work and Grandpa Joe wasn't around. It's true, there were some good times when dad felt well and was working, but we never knew in advance how things would be. Also, the fact that dad was okay in the morning when we'd be having breakfast and getting ready for school didn't necessarily mean that he would be feeling well by the time we came home in the afternoon. It was practically impossible to make any predictions. More than anything else, it was the tension of not knowing how dad would behave at any given moment that riddled us with anxiety on a daily basis. To avoid disappointment and unnecessary anguish, I think that we had both developed intricate defense mechanisms to protect ourselves from being hurt by dad's behavior. Our method was to assume that dad was in bad shape unless proven otherwise. Thus, we would come home from school every day expecting the very worst, with dad locked in his room and not speaking to any of us. If this wasn't the case, we would begin to communicate with him cautiously, proceeding very deliberately, in case we should suddenly find that dad would become depressed and abandon us again for his own lonely and unhappy closed little world.

At any rate, both Ervin and I felt the tension coming home from school each day. We would often try to delay the inevitable and spend our after school hours at the hockey rink. Then, we would saunter home towards dinner, when mom and Grandpa Joe were often present to balance out the delicate situation. We were both a little scared to be left alone with dad.

Although Ervin was only eleven years old, he had a good rapport with the university student whose job was to take care of our neighborhood outdoor hockey rink. Ervin would help Pete clear the snow off the ice on weekends and spend lots of time jabbering hockey talk with him. Ervin knew exactly what he was doing; in return, he managed to wangle a key for the little cabin shack so that we could get out for a skate even on Pete's off-hours, after eight p.m. Monday through Friday and after six p.m. on Saturdays and Sundays. The shack was not only necessary for changing from winter snow boots into skates, but it also controlled the lights for the outdoor rink. This way, Ervin found an alternative solution to our being at home right after school and even later in the evenings. Ultimately, these retreats to the skating rink led to Ervin's prowess as a hockey player and his love of the game, which he maintains to this day.

Cindy had to develop alternative strategies. Being the youngest, mom and dad spoiled her badly. Cindy had an arsenal of dolls and toys that could have filled a small apartment. None of us knew it yet, but such a small apartment would eventually be one of the factors that helped Cindy "hatch" out of her spoiled and protected egg.

In addition to being somewhat spoiled, Cindy possessed a rather violent temper. Any minor infraction with Ervin or occasional skirmish with me would lead to a major temper tantrum. These episodes could last several hours, and they included a variety of special effects such as the slamming of doors, the throwing of anything available in the vicinity (a different Lladró vase than the one I once demolished was once a prime object), and very loud screaming and bawling. Her screams could shake birds' nests out of treetops, even in the winter with the windows closed. Ervin enjoyed provoking these little tantrums. He would set his stopwatch to time how long it would take to induce such a temper tantrum and try to get me to compete with him in guessing how long it would take. Obviously, none of these incidents were particularly helpful with regards to dad's health. Ervin instigated most of these troubles while both mom and Grandpa Joe were away, which greatly complicated matters for me. I did not feel particularly qualified to serve as the U.N. Often I tried to restrain Ervin, but Cindy could be coerced into her violent temper tantrums very easily. Other times, I would try in vain to teach Cindy to ignore Ervin's taunting. This was wholly unsuccessful, because if Ervin couldn't get a rise out of Cindy (which was extremely unusual), he would go after me until I would end up chasing him around the house. He would usually plan his tiresome and relentless attacks on me while I was in my room reading, listening to the radio, or even doing schoolwork now and then. Ervin knew just how to be bothersome; he would hammer on my door or call me names and then run swiftly to his room and lock the door from the inside. To actually catch him, I had two options. One way was to wait until he became desperately bold and took risks by continually knocking on my door. This allowed me to wait close on my side of the door and get near enough to him to occasionally catch him in the act. My other choice was to chase him to his own room, get out a book, and sit by his door keeping him under curfew for hours. This technique was especially effective if there was a hockey game on television. Locked in his room under siege, Ervin would miss the game.

Cindy made friends easily and spent many of her after school hours over at the homes of these friends. In fact, she often slept over with her girlfriends, even on school nights. Mom seemed to think that this wouldn't hurt, and that she would get a chance to be with girls her own age and avoid the combined pressures at home. I agreed, although I often envied her these outlets that were not really available to Ervin and me.

Despite the severity of that particular winter, the frigid climate would prove to be a fitting atmosphere for a far greater tragedy than that of the weather itself. One cold clear Regina afternoon, Ervin and I came home from school to find dad cleaning up the house. We were both very surprised, since he had spent the past several weeks secluded in his room, rarely venturing out at all. We had not seen him at breakfast, and Grandpa Joe had been spending the evenings with us, cooking dinners and helping out as usual. Dad had obviously not been working at his administrative post in Grandpa Joe's factory for some time now. Suddenly, Ervin and I found dad vacuuming the living room carpet, with rock music blaring away on the radio. Dad was even humming along with the music. We both knew that dad hated rock music. When he was feeling well he would frequently complain that very few people appreciated music, which in his view was only classical music. Ervin looked at me and made a sort of sign indicating with his hands that dad had gone crazy. Ervin used his cynical jokes as his mechanism to avoid emotional harm. Before we could get our winter boots off, dad was all over us, "Hey boys, how goes it?"

Dad was now energetically vacuuming the dust off the coffee table in the living room, tossing little statues up in the air and catching them behind his back. I quickly thought to myself, if one more Lladró vase gets broken, mom really will leave us all. Dad was still showing off, the music blaring from the living room speakers. Dad shut the vacuum off and bounced into the kitchen, "Hungry, boys?"

He picked up three eggs out of the refrigerator and began juggling them smoothly. I could see how fragile those eggs were, and I feared the possibility of each cracking open all over the kitchen tiles. "Please, dad," I begged. "Don't do that. They'll break."

"Trust me," he said, "everything's fine now. Things are going to be different around here. We're going to be moving up in the world."

At that point, I didn't know what dad meant. From a completely physical-geographical standpoint, dad's statement would turn out to be an ironically prophetic vision, although I doubt that either his declaration or the final result were really under his control. What I did know was that something was very wrong. It's true that we had been exposed to the occasional short but very energetic manic phase of dad's illness, but we had become far more used to the long, consistent depressive phases. Although I should have known that this was another of dad's symptoms, perhaps the most difficult of them to witness, nothing could have prepared me for this.

"Come on, boys. Get your coats on. Let's go out for a hamburger!"

Ervin cheered. He, too, should have known better. My mistake was not calling mom at the hospital or Grandpa Joe. We shouldn't have gone with him. But neither of us wanted to be the cause of dad's unhappiness and another lengthy retreat to his room.

Dad trudged out to the garage without bothering to take a jacket. "It's not all that cold out," he observed. "They always exaggerate on the radio." It was thirty-three below zero. Celsius. Not that it matters much; I think that the Fahrenheit and Celsius scales intercept at about minus forty, so it's almost the same thing. "Go get my keys, Ervin, they're on my bedroom dresser."

I sat shivering in the frozen Oldsmobile, partly from the cold, but mainly from my hesitancy in not knowing what to do. "Dad, don't you think we should wait for mom. She might be home soon."

"Mom? She'll be at the hospital for hours. By the time she gets home we'll be ready for pizzas." I was old enough to see that the rational approach was not going to help me very much.

Ervin came back with the keys and dad drove rapidly through the icy streets. He skidded and fishtailed along the slippery roads, alternating between braking and accelerating, pumping away on the brakes to avoid colliding with the cars in front of him. Ervin cheered dad on, yelling out, "Floor it, dad!" My swift kicks aimed at Ervin's ankles were clearly not understood. At eleven years of age he was too young to comprehend that this was dangerous and not simply fun and games. I later realized that age was only a minor factor in the comprehension of mental illness. Many adults cannot manage to fathom that mental illness can influence behavior; that such erratic behavior is almost inseparable from the patient's own character. Even rational adults are locked in a state of denial regarding this issue. An educated scientist can still find it hard to come to terms with the idea that we are all delicate balances of chemicals and that the slightest upset in this balance for any reason can tip the scales towards pathological behavior, depression, anxiety, and/or mental instability—all due to a lack or excess of one or more chemicals floating around in our bloodstream or central nervous system. It's no wonder that

Ervin egged dad on. Not that it would have mattered. Dad would have driven on whatever our reactions had been.

Fortunately, we arrived intact at Zeppelin's, the fast food hamburger joint that had been taking western Canada by storm, literally, that winter. Dad said, "Let's eat in the car and order at the drive-in."

"Dad, it's really cold out. Can't we go in? It'll be hard to eat with our jackets and gloves on," I virtually begged him.

"Alright, let's go in." Dad was already jumping out of the door and heading toward the restaurant. I took the time and trouble to remove the keys from the ignition and to lock the car doors, with Ervin trailing after dad. We sat down at a booth with dad bringing us each a double "puff-burger," fries, and a coke without bothering to ask. He ordered three double puff-burgers, fries, onion rings, and a coke for himself. I hadn't even managed to get the wrapper off of mine, and dad had already wolfed down his first burger. I assumed that he really didn't eat much during those long bouts in his room; suddenly, in the booth across from me I envisioned a large grizzly bear, hungrily stocking up for a long hibernation.

The daydream wore off quickly, and I excused myself and headed for the toilets. I went straight for the public telephone, tossed in a quarter and called Grandpa Joe. "Hello," came across his accented voice.

"Grandpa Joe," I greeted him, breathing nervously, "something's happened!" I explained to him where we were and told him of my fears about driving with dad in this condition. "Stay right vere you are. Eat slowly," said Grandpa Joe. "I be right there."

When Grandpa Joe arrived, dad made a bit of a scene, but Grandpa Joe was his father after all. Dad finally agreed to get in Grandpa Joe's car, and I know that mom and Grandpa Joe later picked up dad's car from the restaurant parking lot. I also remember Dr. Roifman visiting us at home, apparently convincing dad to take some kind of pills to settle him down a little. He did seem to calm down for a few days. But he hated taking the pills—they slowed him down—and he must have decided to fool everyone by only pretending to take them for several days.

Time has a way of mesmerizing us, of distorting our memories and selectively impairing them. I can remember vividly the sequences of events that followed, the people involved, even the atmosphere and how I felt. What I fail to remember is precisely when they occurred in reference to the incident at Zeppelin's burgers; it could have been one week, two weeks, or perhaps even five weeks later. Thinking back twenty-five years ago, the exact length of this time span really isn't all that important. In a long talk with mom and Paul recently, she claimed that it was actually only five days later. However, I have noticed that her memory also appears selective with regard to time and dates, possibly her personal protective mechanism to escape from her own guilt.

Whether it was five days or thirty-five days, dad went back into his shell after the incident at Zeppelin's for a period of time. I suppose that the pills he was given were repressing those manic urges that had been boiling up within him. One cold January afternoon I came home from school to find Grandpa Joe's car parked in front of the house. When I entered the front door, I could see that mom was also home. Her car must have been parked in the garage. Together with mom and Grandpa Joe, Uncle Sheldon was also sitting in the living room. Uncle Sheldon was mom's older brother, a senior partner in the largest law firm in Regina. I didn't know Uncle Sheldon very well; he was always working. From the little that I knew, though, I liked him. He always induced confidence and security. I occasionally envied my cousins Richard and Jack, having a father whom they could look up to. They greeted me, but I could tell that something had happened; they had been speaking in hushed voices. Mom also held a drink in her hand, which was most unusual.

"Is something wrong?" I asked cautiously, as I removed my heavy snow boots.

Grandpa Joe turned to me, "Vy don't you go get something to eat? Ve'll come and explain later. Don't vorry. Everything vill be okay."

Mom looked at Grandpa Joe and Uncle Sheldon and said, "Let him stay and hear. He's not a child."

I sat down on the sofa beside Grandpa Joe, who immediately began fondling my hair, and asked, "How vas school?"

"Never mind school, grandpa. What's going on?"

"Let's put it this way," said mom, measuring each word carefully, "your father was feeling badly. Very badly. Remember how dad was acting when he took you to Zeppelin's with Ervin?"

"Of course I remember," I said not wanting to be treated like a child. "He was in what you call his manic phase."

"That's right," mom encouraged, "exactly."

I could see that Uncle Sheldon was shifting in his easy chair, steeling himself for the revelation of the bad news. By the time I had come home, the triumvirate of mom, Grandpa Joe, and Uncle Sheldon had already assessed the immediate damage and they were now striving to understand the ramifications. However, someone would have to explain the damage to me, with or without the future implications.

"Well what's wrong?" I was beginning to lose my cool. "You're acting as though this is the first time. We all know that dad's not well. What else is new?" I said resentfully.

Uncle Sheldon leaned forward and put a hand on my shoulder. "You're a big guy now, so we're going to be honest with you Steve. Your dad went on one of his manic phases, as you correctly described it, and lost a lot of money gambling."

Perhaps I was unusually grown-up for my age, but I still didn't see the problem. It hadn't hit me yet that this could possibly happen. "So," I retorted, "the odds weren't with him today. So what?"

"Steve," mom took over, "your dad lost a tremendous amount of money, far more than we have available."

I looked up at Uncle Sheldon. "How can that be legal, Uncle Sheldon, to win money from a sick man? It's not right."

Uncle Sheldon looked crestfallen. He put his hand back on my shoulder. "You're absolutely right, Steve, it isn't fair. Unfortunately, there's a loophole in the law and it doesn't look like we'll be able to get the money back. At this point, I think we'd all better get used to the idea that there may need to be some temporary changes in our lives."

I looked back to mom and Grandpa Joe. "What does he mean, 'get used to the changes'?"

Mom took the responsibility of informing me. To this day I respect her for finally telling me, flat out. "Steve, dad's debts are so large, he owes so much money, that I'm afraid we are going to have to sell the house to pay for them."

"Sell the house?!" I was stunned. I loved that house. I had been born there and had lived there for fourteen years. Each room had its own history. The basement was my own personal domain, a hockey arena, football stadium, Ping-Pong hall, and much, much more. The backyard was our soccer playground, and the basketball hoop on our garage served all summer as the neighborhood basketball court. Rarely an evening went by without a good two-on-two or three-on-three game picking up. Then, there was my room—my own room with my sports equipment and books. How could we move? Where would we go?

"Steve, you are the older one, the responsible one. This is going to be very hard for Ervin and Cindy. I vant you to do your best to help them. It's not going to be easy to get used to," Grandpa Joe appealed to me.

I fought hard to hold back my tears. I couldn't stand the thought of living anywhere else. It suddenly occurred to me that if we needed to sell the house for the money, then we would have little money available for a new place.

I turned to mom. "If we sell the house to use the money to pay for dad's gambling troubles, then where will we get the money from to find another place to live?"

I could see that mom was also on the brink of crying, and Uncle Sheldon could see that too. He tried to explain "Steve, you know what a mortgage is?"

I nodded my head. I knew that was a type of loan from the bank that we paid back over many years to pay for the house, which we had bought all at once. "Well, we tried to see whether we could increase the mortgage and keep possession of the house. Unfortunately, it just wouldn't do. The plan is as follows: We'll sell the house to a company that I work with for a good price. They will not sell the house, but only rent it out for a couple years to another family. Then, in a relatively short time, we hope that our family can manage to save enough money to buy it back from the company. But in the meantime, we'll all have to do our share to save. And that means a little sacrifice from everyone."

That little sacrifice would turn out to be more than two years in a small rented apartment.

CHAPTER EIGHT

The makeshift apartment that we lived in on Taylor Boulevard for more than two years was small, dingy, and badly lit. Even the dark corridors on each floor seemed to have the sort of "mothball odor" that generally reminded me of older people. It was a common practice among old people to fill their closets with naphthalene balls, in an effort to prevent woolen items from being chewed up by moths. I didn't understand exactly where the odor originated from, since there didn't seem to be many elderly people in the building. As much as we were both antitheses to the observation powers of Sherlock Holmes, even Ervin and I noticed that the flat was shabby with cheap furniture and balding carpets. Our living room Nerf baseball doubleheaders, with Ervin sliding hard into the first base sofa cushions, didn't exactly improve the thinning texture of the carpet during those few years. We were forced to share a tiny bedroom with a little window overlooking the back alley. We also had to share a small closet, which Ervin would maintain perpetually in disarray. However, my most pressing problem was not having my own desk or table to work at. When Ervin occupied himself busily categorizing hockey or baseball cards at our desk, I was forced into the kitchen and the realm of Grandpa Joe to do my schoolwork.

To make enough room for all our sports equipment, books, and various possessions (some of which had been transferred temporarily to Uncle Sheldon's house for storage and safekeeping), we now had bunk beds. Ervin, who claimed that he was afraid of heights, took the bottom bunk, while I had to climb the little iron rung ladder every night to get up to the top bunk. Ervin would sometimes drive me crazy, lying beneath me on his back with his legs stretched out, kicking my mattress underneath me. He also enjoyed lobbing a plethora of handy objects at me from below, including hockey pucks, tennis balls, and running shoes. His lack of knowledge of physics prevented him from understanding two very basic rules: one, the force of gravity, which contends that "what goes up must come down," and two, the principle that "every action has an equal and opposite reaction." Sometimes my reactions overshot their mark, surpassing the "equilibrium" point, but they never seemed to discourage Ervin's next attack. Despite these frequent expressions of frustration, Ervin seemed to be taking things quite well. He seemed to have either matured to some degree or had perhaps developed a mild form of melancholy. The days where he would bang on my door and bolt for his own room or the basement seemed to have dissipated. Perhaps this was only due to technical reasons: He no longer had his own room to flee to and there was no longer a basement available for romping around and playing hockey and Ping-Pong. In spite of these drawbacks, Ervin still seemed to have grown up. He was helping out more at home, even making his own lunches. "No more tuna sandwiches!" he said to me once, pleased with himself.

Since we no longer had our domain for basement ball hockey, Nerf football, and other indoor winter sports, except for the rare occasions when only the two of us were home, Ervin and I were forced to develop alternative ways to expend our energy. There was a different neighborhood outdoor ice hockey rink, close to the apartment, that we frequented in the cold winter months, weather permitting. Unfortunately, Gavin, the young student who took care of the skating rink, was less amiable than Ervin's old buddy, Pete, who took care of the rink near where we used to live. At this new rink, Ervin had trouble getting his own key for the dressing shack. To this aim, we formulated an intricate plan that starred the theatrical antics of Suzy, the sixteen-year-old daughter of one of our new apartment neighbors, Mrs. Allbright. Mrs. Allbright shampooed heads for a pair of hair stylists who owned and worked in a downtown beauty salon. She apparently moonlighted by reading horoscopes and telling fortunes. Ervin and I used to joke that one thing was for sure—Suzy's mom certainly wasn't all that bright. Suzy, though, was a good sport and actually a lot of fun to be with. Although she was a couple years older than I was, and much older than Ervin, she was always available for street hockey games out in the back lane, touch football in the summer, and even basketball pickup games at the nearby outdoor courts.

One afternoon, when we were trying to calculate how we could get hold of Gavin's key to the rink dressing shack, I had an idea. "Suzy, you're pretty," I said blushing slightly. Ervin would spend hours kidding me about my feelings for Suzy after *that* episode. "Maybe you could interest Gavin in teaching you to skate around the rink for a while, while we grab the key and run to the shopping center to copy it?"

Surprisingly, Suzy actually liked the idea. To my greater astonishment, I felt a little hurt that she was so willing to go ahead enthusiastically with the plan and spend time with Gavin. I suppose that these were my first twinges of romantic jealousy.

Suzy's performance was superb—straight from the Regina Theater Center. She put on a really terrific act and, faking innocence, asked Gavin to teach her to skate one Saturday afternoon. This, she later claimed, was no simple task for her, because she had taken figure skating lessons for six years and now had to pretend she could barely stand on her ankles. With Gavin out on the ice, busy in his new role as a great skating teacher, Ervin and I had time for the dangerous job ahead. We quickly rifled through the pockets of his jacket, which he left hanging on a hook in the shack. Ervin immediately found some "goodies"; I had to force him to put the package of condoms back in Gavin's pocket. After finally calming my brother down, I could see that we were faced with a problem. Gavin had a key ring with four different keys on it. We did not know which key was the one that opened the shack door, and we couldn't possibly try them with Gavin gliding back and forth only meters away. Ervin and I raced to the nearby hardware store and had to copy all four of them. It turned out that we could have easily stolen his little car or broken into his house, wherever he lived. But that didn't interest us; we only wanted our own key to the shack, and thanks to Suzy, we now had it.

It was another typical prairie winter, with temperatures dipping well below minus thirty degrees Celsius for weeks at a time. Although we now had the key to the neighborhood hockey rink dressing shack, there were still many winter afternoons that were too cold to skate outdoors. Grandpa Joe's car had to have the battery replaced twice during that bitterly cold winter. Two weeks in a row, vandals had removed the exterior car engine heater from the electrical socket in the parking lot during the night, causing all the battery fluids to freeze up. "Communists," Grandpa Joe would mutter, "that's vat they are, communists."

Because the apartment was very cramped, with no privacy for Ervin and me, and with precious little space to maneuver, even when dad was well, we looked for alternative activities outside the apartment. Together with Suzy, Ervin and I would occupy our time for hours and hours, playing a form of "hide and seek," all within the ugly, naphthalene-reeking building complex. Even Suzy enjoyed these childish games; she even once fooled us by camping out and hiding for three hours in the third floor laundry chute. Ervin enjoyed the realm of the building. Although it was little consolation for the loss of our beloved house, the space in the building outside our own actual apartment presented us with the means to stay out of dad's way on those chilling winter evenings. Ervin would go flying up and down the elevators, whizzing in and out emergency exits, and spying on various tenants in the building with his binoculars. I think that he knew that building better than the architect who designed it; he was forever discovering new "secret" staircases, walk-in cupboards with stairways, and routes underground where the parking lot was stationed. Sometimes, Suzy and I would let him hide for hours "to get rid of him," so to speak.

Although I was only fourteen at the time, and Suzy was nearly sixteen, I began to feel that she was showing unusual interest in me. She was almost a full head taller than me, with broad shoulders and developed breasts that wiggled as she ran down the hall. She was not pretty, but had a certain appeal to her, with her almost-voluptuous, well-rounded body and childlike foolery. At first, she was just another player in whatever game we were playing. Slowly I began to notice that I would be thinking of Suzy at nights before falling asleep. Then I realized that there were nights when my thoughts of Suzy were perhaps *preventing* me from falling asleep. However, I could not seem to grasp how Suzy could possibly be interested in *me*, who was a grade below her in school, almost two years younger, and not even her size. If we were standing beside each other, at best I looked like her kid brother. I also knew that Suzy was popular at school; she had many girlfriends as well as several boyfriends, some of whom she would tell me about. Sometime that winter Suzy described to me how a guy she had met at a party had "made a pass" at her. She seemed to revel in describing to me all the gory details, whose lips were where, how his hands slid under her shirt and unhooked her bra. I think she was testing me then, to see if I was mature enough or interested enough in her. I continued to dream lustfully of Suzy that winter, using her image to escape from that cramped apartment and to bury myself within my imagination and locate my own private place where neither dad's illness nor Ervin could get to me.

That spring, when the huge piles of grayish snow finally

began to thaw, we moved our hide-and-seek games to the great outdoors. One warm summer-like evening, it was Ervin's turn to find us. Suzy grabbed my hand and whispered, "Come on, let's go to the park." Suzy led me to the small wooded park near our house, an area that was not supposed to be within the range of our game. She sensed my thoughts, "Never mind Ervin. Let him look for us." We eventually arrived at a very small clearing surrounded from all sides by tall, thick shrubs and a few towering elms. From outside the little clearing, no one (aside from Suzy, who I later understood had been there before) could possibly guess that there was a grassy patch with absolute privacy in the middle of the park. Before I could think what was happening, Suzy had tackled me to the ground and was sliding her tongue into my mouth. My first reaction could be described as a "gut reaction"; I almost retched. Suzy hadn't even bothered to spit out her fat wad of bubble gum, and the smell of it now almost in my mouth had my stomach muscles tensed and poised for the worst. But I did not want to hurt her feelings. Perhaps more importantly, I had the feeling that there was more to come and that things would soon improve. This feeling was not solely an imaginary or hopeful wish. It was firmly based on the fact that she was sliding one hand under my shirt and stroking my chest while the other was simultaneously pulling my own shaky and inexperienced hand underneath her own blouse, inducing me to feel the smooth flesh of her own well-rounded breasts. Contending with my utter lack of any previous experience, I valiantly managed not to gag from her bubble gum and followed her lead. Before long I could feel that stirring of passion that grips me up until this day when I think of Suzy (and other women for that matter). Suzy was no awkward newcomer to this kind of operation. From her clever choice of the secluded location, to the rapid unzipping of my jeans, and on to the speedy removal of her own clothes, Suzy knew what she was doing. Her coordinated hands also knew exactly what to do with me, as well as what to do to herself for her own satisfaction. I certainly had no idea at the time. Upon finally catching my breath and recovering from Suzy's expert manual dexterity, I did manage to watch as she eventually brought relief to herself, somewhat noisily. I half-panicked; I was afraid that someone passing by through the park would hear her. No one did. In the upcoming months, Suzy would no longer have to rely solely on her own prowess to obtain her sexual gratification.

During the year, Suzy Allbright and I would have ample time to experiment together. Our little encounters became very important to us both. In the winter, we would often utilize her apartment bedroom when her mother was out telling fortunes. If Mrs. Allbright was at home, we would turn up the volume of Suzy's tape deck on the pretext of listening to music to prevent her mother from hearing us. While Suzy continued to go out with many different boys and was always a popular girl at school (who wouldn't be seen with a "little shrimp" like me), she seemed just as eager to pursue these sexual outings as I was. For me, these meetings were an unbelievable dream; not only did they fill me with hope and anticipation, but they presented a relief-filled escape from both the situation at home and my worsening social problems at school. I was having a terrible time. I was un-popular and treated as a social reject. I was the type who girls would never go out with. Suddenly, I was given this amazing opportunity to mature. I was no longer affected by the silly little sexual cracks that my schoolmates constantly made. My facial expressions at school had once registered my unhappiness when the guys would laugh at my virginity or lack of sexual experi-ence. But now, even my spiteful schoolmates seemed to notice that this no longer affected me. "Leave him alone," ordered Rick, the ringleader. "That fag is so queer he probably gets off standing on his head and meditating."

But I didn't care anymore; I knew that all the boasts of sexual conquests made by Rick and the others were silly attempts to prove their manhood. These were simply macho instincts. I felt relieved; I had my own real sexual encounters, and I had no need to share them with anyone, except Suzy, of course.

Although I fully understood that these meetings were temporary, a trial period that would wear off as Suzy eventually turned
to bigger and better youths, I was perfectly satisfied with the
arrangement. I remembered my pangs of jealousy watching her
skate with Gavin the shack keeper but was astute enough to realize that Suzy was only a stepping stone for me. I liked her very
much and generally enjoyed our mutually pleasurable physical
contact, except for the bubble gum, of course. However, I often
felt that once we had each achieved our physical satisfactions,
there was not a lot left in common between us. Suzy didn't read
books, and I could never explain to her how things were at home
in the apartment or at school. She didn't seem interested. At the
same time, I blanked my mind whenever she began to talk to me
about one party or another or some high school football player
who asked her out. She found it important to assure me that
even the best looking football players didn't receive her attentions and manipulations like I did, at least not right away. Unlike
me, though, she lacked the sensitivity to realize that I just didn't
care. Still, we kept up our meetings faithfully, as they were still
beneficial to us both.

The apartment years, or the "apartment phase" as mom
would eventually resort to psychological lingo to depict them,
served as difficult times for all of us children at school. Cindy
quickly learned that many of her former friends were snubbing
her, refusing to come to her new apartment home, and becoming less and less willing to invite her to their own extravagant
houses. Ervin had always been somewhat of a loner, and now
seemed even more absorbed in listening to his short-wave radio
and roaming the apartment building for hours and hours. Those
years were also marked by tremendous attempts by mom and
Grandpa Joe, together with help from Uncle Sheldon, to save
money. We children knew little about what went on behind the
scenes—the extra hours Mom put in working overtime at the
hospital and the shares of his company that Grandpa Joe sold
to keep us going. Ervin and I did notice that mom seemed less

aware of our clothes and running shoes. Ervin would wear my old clothes although they were often a size too large. I would wear hand-me-downs from Uncle Sheldon's boys; some of them looked like they hadn't even been worn before. None of this bothered either of us. However, the situation was far more difficult for Cindy. The sudden drop from queen to drone, the loss of social status, was a major blow to her. Unlike us, Cindy was obsessively aware of her appearance, particularly her clothes. Ervin's hand-me-downs were not considered "acceptable" by either Cindy or her girlfriends. Cindy came home from school crying shrilly one afternoon and informed us that the kids had been calling her "refugee Cindy." She didn't know what that meant, but she could tell by the teasing tones of her classmates that it was not meant as a compliment. Although she did not know it at the time, Cindy's experiences during these years would ultimately shape her future. The "apartment phase" would perhaps save her from a life of eccentric pleasures and help mold a woman with an established social conscience. Mom would later claim that dad's financial mess may have had more of a positive impact on our lives of us than anything else he did. Perhaps she was right.

Ervin and I, despite our lack of concern about our clothes and appearance, also had peer trouble to contend with at school. The story about dad losing our savings gambling was spread around together with a number of vicious lies. One afternoon, on the way home from school, Ervin suddenly asked me, "What's a whore?"

"Where did you hear that?" I asked him curiously. He was a little young at the time to fully comprehend the finer aspects of that type of vocation, anyway.

"Mike said that mom became a whore so that dad can pay off what he lost gambling."

"Tell Mike," I dictated to Ervin slowly, "that if he ever mentions mom again, your older brother is going to break every bone in his body. And forget what he said. It's just a silly story he made up."

I myself also had to put up with a lot of goading. That didn't bother me too much, especially since I was now spending a great deal of time with Suzy. Our odd relationship helped build up my confidence and I realized that within a few years I wouldn't have to see any of these schoolmates any more. I understood that soon I would meet new people, more "Suzys" who wouldn't care where I lived and how much money my family had. I was an unusually good student, and this apparently worsened matters by serving as a source of jealousy, often leading to more attempts to humiliate me. I developed a very sharp tongue and spared even the biggest bullies no cracks. I was not afraid to hit back. However, there was an additional problem; if only verbal violence and being cursed were the most severe forms of attack, I would have been fine. Unfortunately, there were occasional physical attacks to cause me to "atone" for my "lack of respect." One time, after heartily congratulating Rick, the leader of the bullies, for receiving 5% on an algebra exam (the teacher gave him a bonus for spelling his name correctly), he tried to take revenge. During a break between classes, Rick and three of his cronies dragged me into the washroom. "Let's give him a whirly," suggested one of them. That was the name of the procedure where one's head is forcibly propelled into a toilet, which is then flushed. The only thing more disgusting than a whirly is a "chocolate" whirly, which I will leave to the imagination. I fought valiantly, getting in a good kick at Rick's vital parts, which left him gasping for air, blue in the face on the washroom floor. However, that only incensed his henchmen and increased their motivation; they pinned my arms and forced me into the toilet stall. I was saved by the prostate of old Mr. Peabody, the vice-principal, who walked in to do his business just in the nick of time. Being well equipped to advocate my own position compared with the tongue-tied henchmen and Rick, who was still gasping for oxygen, I managed to extricate myself from the mess and get the henchmen and Rick into some serious trouble. Throughout the year, they would manage to do me a number of evils, but they never did succeed in giving me a whirly. My coincidental association with a leather-jacketed tough guy by the name of Micky Morooney would soon change my status among my schoolmates. Little did I imagine at that time the effect that Micky Morooney would eventually have on my entire family more than twenty years later.

Micky Morooney was big for his age. He was a tall youth, sturdily built, with greasy black hair. He sported a thick moustache, unusual at our age, as further proof of his having successfully reached puberty. Actually, he was at least a year older than the rest of the kids in my class. I never did quite understand how many grades he had been kept back. Morooney was known by his many enemies and rivals as "The Moron" and by his admirers as "The Meat Grinder." He was not in any of my classes; in fact I practically didn't even know him, but everybody knew *about* him. Morooney had been suspended and expelled a number of times from various schools. It seemed to be in his blood. He had cursed teachers and principals, burned textbooks during class, lit stink bombs in the classrooms, and urinated in his desk. It was rumored that he had been expelled from his previous high school for locking a teacher in his classroom *by welding the door shut.*

Morooney never went anywhere without his tight, black leather jacket, in winter or summer. It was as though he had no body temperature of his own. Perhaps that jacket provided him with his own private self-sufficient ecosystem, like those suits used by the volunteer scientists in the Biosphere 2 bubble built out in the Arizona desert. Another rumor held that Morooney never went anywhere without his personal, customized, six inch switchblade, with his initials engraved on the handle. His most recent claim to fame was a rather unique method for expressing his displeasure with a certain trigonometry formula. He had simply walked up to the blackboard after class and calmly smashed his fist through the chalked formula on the board. The next day he arrived at school with a nice new plaster cast on his right arm.

One stormy winter afternoon, as I sat in my final class for the day, I knew that I was in real trouble. Rick and at least two of his fellow bullies were also present in that class. Usually, on those Tuesdays, to avoid trouble, I would extract my jacket and possessions from my locker in the hall prior to the literature class and find a seat as near to the door as possible. When class ended, I could easily outrun beefy Rick and his henchmen and slip out of the school to one of the nearby bus stops. However, Mr. Horyniuk, my biology teacher, had detained me after the previous lesson to discuss my science research project, and I didn't have time to collect my belongings from my locker before the literature class without being late. So, there I sat in English literature, with *Hamlet* being the least of my worries. "To be or not to be" was a philosophical question that contained multiple meanings for me. I weighed my available possibilities carefully. One of them was to bolt straight for the door as soon as the final bell rang, ignoring my locker with my coat and backpack in it. The idea was to try to surprise and thus lose them. This solution contained two particularly problematic drawbacks. The minor one was that my wallet, with money for the bus, was in the locker. That was okay. I was willing to walk home—or even run if necessary. The major problem was my winter jacket; it was eighteen below zero outside. I began to calculate the various risks involved: pneumonia versus broken ribs, hospitalization in the Department of Internal Medicine versus the Orthopedic Department. Neither option was particularly comforting to me, even if mom was a doctor. Another option that skirted through my mind was the possibility of engaging Mrs. Connell in a fascinating discussion about "recurrent foreshadowing in Shakespeare's plays" or some other "dodgy" issue (as Nigel would say) in order to exit the class in her protective custody. However, chances were that they would follow from a distance and pounce on me as soon as she entered the teachers' lounge to get her own coat before leaving the school. We students were not allowed in the teachers' lounge. When the bell tolled ("for whom it tolled" was unfortunately me in this instance), I still had not devised a concrete plan. I decided to simply play cool and hope that they'd overlook me. I set out for my locker unobstructed, but immediately after donning my jacket and locking the locker, I found myself surrounded by Rick and his cronies.

"You little ass licker, you're in shit now! This time we're going to show you what happens to fucking little geeks like you who snitch on classmates," raved Rick, to the taunts and cheers of his followers.

I could see that in this predicament nothing I could say or do was going to change things anyway, so I let loose myself. They were definitely going to kick me around, but I was determined not to let them see my fear nor enjoy my ruin. I also figured that if I could maneuver them into a situation where it wasn't four against one, my chances of coming out alive would be better. I ignored the cronies and spoke directly to Rick Cobbs, the leader. "You're some tough guy. You need three bodyguards to help you beat me up. What're you afraid that I'll pound your head in if you don't have help? I don't know why your chums bother with you. They must sense that you're a wimp!"

That was a dangerous opening. On his order, they could have all begun hacking me apart piece by piece. However, my psychology appeared to be accurate, at least at the start. Apparently, I didn't inherit my psychological prowess from Mom's side of the family. Rick Cobbs felt threatened; his honor was at stake, although there was certainly no chance of his losing a fight to me. He was almost a full head taller than I was and must have weighed twenty-five to thirty pounds more than I did. I waved "hello" to an imaginary friend behind him and made a sudden surprise charge at his legs, startling him and knocking him to the ground. That was a good start, because except for one or two swift kicks that my ribs absorbed from his friends while we were still rolling around on the floor, I was actually fighting one instead of four. It took a good few minutes until Rick managed to get the upper hand and crawled on top of me, pounding away at my face with his fists. I could taste my own blood; I wasn't sure whether it was from a cut in my lip or my eye or both, but I was still not entirely beaten and even managed the odd swing at his head, which was blurring rapidly and beginning to resemble that of a Siamese twin. Either that or I was seeing double. Suddenly, from out of nowhere, something grabbed Rick's neck, lifting his entire weight off of me, and slammed him head first into the locker. I heard a dull thud as Rick's head dented the locker and could sense the slithering sound of his limp body gliding to the floor. Despite my half-delirious state, I knew that Rick would no longer be in shape to continue my beating. I looked up and saw the Morooney "twins," or at least he looked like twins. He looked around at Rick's buddies, who were inching away from me, and declared in a deep voice, "Any-fucking-body who fucking touches him fucking dies." That was all he said. That was all he needed to say. My shocked attackers backed away, trembling with fear, dragging their wounded leader with them. Morooney had a distinctive manner of speaking; he was unable or unwilling to stretch two consecutive syllables without the infamous f-word in between. In fact, when there was an occasional need for utilizing multisyllabic words, Morooney found it necessary to split the word into distinct syllables in order to insert the f-word in the middle, hence "any-fucking-body." Stories circulated discussing how this unusual habit could not be broken, even in class in conversations with teachers. At any rate, at this point I simply didn't care who he was and what his reasons were; all I knew was that he may well have saved me from the hospital. As it turned out, Morooney didn't arbitrarily decide to help me out. A year earlier, his father had developed a malignant growth in his throat. After the oncologists had removed his dad's tumor, my mom had operated on him and had managed to save or repair his dad's vocal chords. After my fight with Rick, Morooney put out word that he would personally "dis-fucking-able" anyone who bothered me. No one ever touched me or even threatened me again in that school. Years later, I would joke with mom that she was not the typical protective type of Jewish mother, but she sure knew how to obtain protection when it was needed.

CHAPTER NINE

During those unforgettably rough years in the cramped, rented Regina apartment, Grandpa Joe could not have possibly have been more supportive than he was. He was a ghost-like presence, constantly hovering and roving about everywhere. He continually encouraged us, spreading his everlasting optimism like margarine on toast. He helped keep the peace between us and kept our hopes up for dad's health and for moving back to our former house. Grandpa Joe spent virtually all of his spare time with us. He dusted, cleaned, vacuumed, and even cooked dinners and lunches. Simply by being there, he served as an educator and a big brother. During this time, Grandpa Joe was also preoccupied at his factory. Although he sold shares from his company to help bail us out financially, the profits gained from these manipulations turned out to be insufficient. Dad's gambling debts were very deep indeed. Uncle Sheldon, who has remained in sporadic contact with me over the years, recently revealed to me how he had exerted his substantial influence in pulling strings to avoid having dad's creditors repossess all of our possessions at the Wascana Drive house. Uncle Sheldon, together with Grandpa Joe, had managed to hold off the hordes of money lenders from carting off our television, our stereo, and perhaps even our sports equipment. That would have been a particularly frightening experience for us children. Mom added to the tale by telling me how she and Uncle Sheldon had managed to cut off dad's credit card and take his checkbooks from him after the incident. In addition to long, tiring days and evenings with us in the apartment, Grandpa Joe began to put in nights at his factory office in an attempt to formulate ways to earn money faster. He was moderately successful, but with the severity of our debts, I understand that we were lucky even to have the little apartment and not to be scrambling out on the streets, fighting for park benches with the shopping bag ladies.

Despite the tremendous and much appreciated goodwill of Grandpa Joe, it seems fair to claim that the greatest sacrifice made during those years was by mom. I learned this many years later from the story that I managed to piece together like a giant jigsaw puzzle after interrogating both mom and Paul on a number of separate occasions. Mom also realized that Grandpa Joe's factory earnings, including royalties from some of his stocks, together with some generous help from Uncle Sheldon would not be enough to allow us to buy back the house for many years if they were not supplemented with additional income. Mom began working nights, weekends, and holidays at the hospital and at several private clinics to enhance her earnings. We hardly saw her, and although we knew she was doing her best to extricate us from our predicament, her lack of availability and accessibility sorely hurt us.

However, the most significant sacrifice that mom made was staying and living with us in the apartment, even though we rarely saw her. The relationship between mom and dad had deteriorated so completely and was so utterly wretched that they had almost nothing left in common to talk about, even during those rare phases where dad was communicative. Years later, mom described to me how she had felt a desperate need to leave the apartment and how difficult it had become to continue living under the same roof with dad. Yet, she had pledged not to leave us children until she (together with Grandpa Joe and Uncle Sheldon) had set us back on our feet and moved us back to our own familiar Wascana Drive home. Mom felt that the trauma created by dad's gambling debts together with his ongoing illness and the loss of our home would be too overwhelming for us if coupled with the loss of her presence too. Her absence at this stage, though, would have been primarily a psychological one since she wasn't around much anyway. Nevertheless, she remained rooted in her own rotten life and stayed with us in the cramped apartment until her goal of moving us back to our old house had been accomplished.

At the time, mom was an attractive woman of about forty. She had a plain but pretty face, with strong features and bright eyes. We all loved mom, but she was certainly not a typical mother. At least she was very different from the mothers of the other children who went to school with me; it was not just her career, but her manner with us. Her patience and comfort was crucial to us all during those difficult years. Each evening on those nights where she wasn't on call at the hospital, we anticipated her arrival anxiously. I will never forget the level of tension on those evenings even if I live 100 years and Alzheimer's disease blunts out the rest of my conscious existence. Mom was a kind person and almost eternally calm with that knowledge of just what to do in every situation. At least that's what radiated from her. Little did I know at the time what tremendous forces were welling up within her, ready to spout like active geysers in the early hours of dawn; powerful tectonic plates were cracking the very core of her foundations. And at the surface, only the calm, implacable, shatterproof exterior was on display for us children.

Mom claims that the first time she met Paul was one of the many times when she was working all night at the hospital in her Ear, Nose, and Throat department (or the ENT as it was known). The ENT was not an especially large department, and it was usually sufficient to leave one specialist there "on call" night and weekends. Normally, specialists like mom, who had already accumulated more than ten years of experience and were considered leading ENT experts in the city, were not required to do "extra duty" at the hospital. Such extra duty included nights, weekends, and holidays. The newly graduated specialist residents were usually left to manage on their own, with an emergency phone number of a more experienced ENT in case there was something particularly difficult to deal with. There were no scheduled ENT operations at night or on weekends. Mom, however, was doing everything humanly possible to help earn more money, so that we could eventually buy back our much beloved home. She would later admit to me that perhaps that was not her only motivation. By her own recount, it was possible that she was using this as an excuse to get away from dad. At the time, though, she was certain of her altruistic intentions in working long days and nights.

Paul was an orthopedic surgeon at the same hospital. He was a few years older than mom, recently widowed, and his sixteen-year-old daughter, Delia, was still living with him—at least in theory. Delia was a continual source of problems for Paul, even from the time when her mother, Paul's wife Ann, had still been alive. Mom always steadfastly maintained that Delia's problem was primarily based on "only-child syndrome," but as I have noted before, a developed sense and understanding of psychology did not rate among mom's more refined abilities. Delia was a "punk rocker." By the time she had turned fourteen, she had bright green hair that stood up as though she had just stuck her finger in an electric socket. But she hadn't, Paul would note wryly; he thought that perhaps if she had, that might have shocked some sense into her. Delia always wore a black leather jacket that wouldn't have shamed even Micky Morooney, and her closet contained a store of very odd clothes. One garment that was particularly hard for Paul to deal with was a T-shirt with a high quality close-up of a woman's breasts localized exactly to that strategic region of the shirt. Moreover, the shirt was skin pink, leaving the impression from even fairly close up that Delia was not wearing a shirt. Years later Paul would admit that he suspected that the close-up photograph of the breasts on Delia's shirt actually exhibited her own mammary glands, but of course Paul would never have asked her. Delia was also a big partygoer; she would be "chaperoned" to all-night parties by big eighteen year olds with hairy faces and noisy motorcycles. Paul simply didn't know what to do with her. She had always been associated with what Paul had called "the underlife," even while Ann was alive, but since her death things had taken a turn for the worse. Thus it came to be that Paul was also busy at the hospital, working nights in the orthopedic department when he, too, was really past that stage of his life. He felt that he was doing penitence for his rotten turn in life, but like mom, he was also trying to run away from problems at home that he couldn't face. Thinking back to those times, I thought to myself, what a bunch of lucky ENT and orthopedic residents having doctors like mom and Paul to ease their heavy loads!

Apparently, one night at the hospital, mom was on the fourth floor on a slow evening, making herself coffee at three a.m., when she was called down to the emergency room. That was the main reason for mom being there, as there were no night operations and not much to do in the ward. She came down the elevator and entered the emergency ward. The head nurse took her aside and said, "I didn't expect you so quickly, Dr. Miller. That's Mrs. Stone over there. She couldn't sleep so she got up and had some chicken to eat and claims that a bone got stuck in her throat. She ran to the sink to get some water and slipped and broke her hip. The intern, Dr. Warren, doesn't think there's anything left wedged in her pharynx, but as soon as Dr. Tate finishes setting the hip, perhaps you should make sure."

Mom looked down and could see Dr. Paul Tate comforting Mrs. Stone—explaining, reassuring, and taking control. To this day, she says that the calm control that Paul displayed with the older patient made her fall for him instantly. She felt that his reassuring presence was something that she badly needed. Until now, she had been at it alone. Grandpa Joe had always helped out, but he was particularly good for us kids. He was biased; he was from dad's side and always would be, right to the end.

From this point on, the story always becomes confused as to who smiled at whom first, but if I had to choose sides and decide whose memory is better, I would elect to go with Paul's reconstruction.

"Your mom walked around to the other side of Mrs. Stone, smiled at me, and then looked at Mrs. Stone and said, 'Hello, Mrs. Stone. I'm Dr. Miller from the Ear, Nose, and Throat department. I can see that you are being looked after well. As soon as Dr. Tate finishes up, I'll take a quick look in your throat to make sure everything's okay.'" Paul claims that mom stressed the "Dr. Tate" a fraction of a second too long, so that it practically rolled off the tip of her tongue waiting for her to get it out. Mom remembers no such emphasis placed on Paul's name.

Another debatable point is who invited whom for coffee in his/her department that night. Whatever the truth regarding the initial invitation, they decided to go up to mom's department, because there was some cake in the refrigerator there. From then on, it was easy to see how the connection developed. Mom and Paul soon began to plan their nightly work schedules together, so that practically every night that they worked, they would be able to talk and have coffee together, time permitting of course. After all, it was a hospital and there were accidents and emergencies, even in Regina. It was my understanding that mom and Paul carried on together, getting to know each other extremely well with long deep conversations, for more than eight months without actually seeing one another away from their working environment. I also assumed that during that time, they formed a deep platonic friendship without actually making their relationship a physical one. Paul was still mourning the loss of his Ann to a horrible colon cancer, and mom was unsure of how to extricate herself from the situation at home. It was not clear whether dad needed her at all, but we children and even Grandpa Joe needed her very much in our present situation. Thinking back, the slow platonic development of mom and Paul's relationship seemed in stark contrast with my own physical association with Suzy, which was going on almost simultaneously. It was also in contrast to Delia's behavior; she was apparently staying out and sleeping with entire rock groups at the time. And she was only sixteen. However, although Paul's frustration with his daughter's situation may have influenced his own behavior, perhaps causing him to retreat as far as possible from Delia's actions, mom certainly did not know about my encounters with Suzy. Obviously, she still doesn't and won't ever know about them. Her own slow and cautious approach to her developing romance with Paul was based entirely on her responsibility for the extremely sensitive situation at home and her will to get us out of the apartment and back to our own house.

The first year, none of us at home had any cause for suspicious thoughts concerning mom's private life. Mom was working harder and harder at the hospital, spending fewer and fewer nights with us in the apartment, and we all assumed that the heavy load she undertook was her way of helping out. In the second year since old Mrs. Stone had broken her hip on that fateful night, mom and Paul finally began seeing each other outside the hospital. Almost immediately, they realized that keeping up the secrecy was becoming increasingly problematic for them both. Paul had continually warned her, "Judy, as soon as we meet outside the hospital, this will get out. It doesn't matter where. It's a small city and there won't be any way to hide it. It would be better if we think this out properly."

Mom had argued, "Let's try for a short time anyway, Paul. I don't care about rumors or what anybody says, but before making a big issue, maybe we should try and see if things work out for us outside the hospital. Maybe they won't." But they both knew that this wasn't true. They had finally found in each other some personal meaning for existence and some real understanding.

At first they met at night only, going to obscure restaurants and dark cafes. Later they began to sleep together at Paul's place. His daughter was rarely there, and even when she was home, she was sleeping, drunk, stoned, or some combination of the three. She didn't represent much of a threat of disclosing their secret relationship. Within a short time, mom began to feel pangs of conscience eating away at her. She was continually searching for rational and moral justifications for her behavior, but to no avail. Here she was, on the pretext of helping out the family, spending more and more time away from us. Paul suggested that she move in with him, but she was adamant that the natural development of her relationship with Paul would have to wait until she and her family had enough money to buy back their former house. Otherwise, she supposed intuitively, the shock of her moving out would be too great for us. Mom's psychology was wrong again. I don't think that the situation could possibly have deteriorated to a state worse than the one that already existed. The tension at home was simply unbearable, and all of us, with the exception of Grandpa Joe, were doing everything in our power to stay away as long as possible, including mom. What she didn't realize was that if she had moved in with Paul without hesitation, the new environment at Paul's home might just have provided the necessary refuge for us three children. Perhaps if we had been exposed to Paul's kind and comforting behavior on weekends or after school while visiting mom there, things might actually have improved greatly for us. Moreover, theoretically at least, if mom had officially disengaged herself from dad back then and had requested custody of the children, she surely would have received it, with or without Paul in the background. We could have all moved in with Paul. Years later, mom would still be very vague about that option, but I knew the reason. Grandpa Joe still hoped for better times and new beginnings in the family, and mom did not want to demolish any remaining hope held by Grandpa Joe. Years and years would go by before she could eventually bring herself to leave the city, despite her divorce from dad and marriage to Paul.

Paul eventually provided the solution that returned us to our old house and, for him at least, no less importantly, finally set mom free of her obligations. He sold his own house and used the money he received to buy a small condominium for himself and mom. Then, he used the money left over to help buy back our Wascana Drive home for the family.

Ervin and Cindy were ecstatic. They were jumping up and down and remembering all the good things about the old house. I had already lost any of the enthusiasm I should have had. My meetings with Suzy were becoming few and far in between, and I was developing stomach cramps before school every morning, a sign that today I recognize in my professional capacity as an indication of anxiety. I was also old enough to sense what was happening. By now I knew that Dr. Paul Tate was a close friend of mom's; just how close, I could only guess. I also knew that he was helping to provide the money for our return to the old status quo. I liked Paul very much, even back then, but I sensed that something in the balance had changed and couldn't help anticipating how it would hit me.

Meanwhile, Grandpa Joe was enraged. Traces of late night conversations wafted to my ears through the thin walls of Ervin's and my room. "How can you take money from this stranger," came the pleading voice of Grandpa Joe, "this Goy? Ven did you meet him? Vat vill happen to the children? Ver is your responsibility? Do you realize vat vill happen to your husband ven he hears?"

I don't remember how mom answered, but Grandpa Joe would never really forgive her. He, too, knew that mom's association with Paul symbolized the end of her relationship with dad. Together with that, for Grandpa Joe at least, this would be the end of our family as he knew it and understood it. His "school" taught that family is family for life, and that one must stick it out through thick and thin. But Grandpa Joe was dad's father and not his wife. He would always be dad's father, but mom would not remain dad's wife. He grasped all these things, but the deflation of his hope for dad's recovery along with that of the family was too great for him to bear. He would maintain this grudge against mom for years and years.

We eventually packed and moved back into our Wascana Drive house, but it just wasn't the same. Mom officially moved in with Paul and never came back to the house to live. Instead, Grandpa Joe moved in with us. The moment that we all had been striving, suffering, and waiting for so long had finally arrived. But we returned to our much desired home wounded and in much worse shape than when we had left it more than two years earlier.

CHAPTER TEN

Mornings are always complicated for me. Although I am an easy riser, popping out from under my quilt as soon as my alarm clock begins to ring with its habitual insolence has never been much fun. To make matters worse, upon hearing the alarm, Compo has a habit of jumping up on the bed and leaning on me with all his weight. I suppose that this is his way of wishing me "good morning." His beefy early morning breath in my face isn't exactly a pleasing odor to awaken to. It reminds me of some of the vile-smelling chemicals in the lab or perhaps Opera-Singh's potent tea. However, I assume that my own breath before brushing my teeth isn't all that pleasant either. Of course, Compo never complains. My coordination remains jittery until I wolf down my first cup of strong expresso. I try to equal Neal's multitasking feats in the lab by making coffee and brushing my teeth simultaneously, but I always end up with toothpaste on my coffee mug or razor stubble on my toast.

On this particular morning, once the espresso warmed my grated throat, I began to feel more capable and even managed to flip through the *Globe and Mail* headlines as Compo led me down the stairs on the way out for his morning "double." Taking leave from Compo with the traditional treat and handshake, and his remorseful snubbing and backing under the table with that pathetic look of his, I propelled myself out into the brisk Ontario air. Every time I closed the door with that dog on the other side, I always felt guilty. I had tried taking him to work once, where he sat on the rug under my desk, but he nearly gave Smithers a heart attack one morning when he knocked on my door to come in and discuss the course that we teach together. Once I get my tenure, I thought to myself, Smithers can stuff himself. The problem is that he's such a sly bastard; behind the scenes he's probably my major adversary, pulling strings against me and slowing down my tenure at the committee workshops.

I headed down to my car and drove cautiously through the snowy Toronto streets. I was in good spirits. After spending long hours writing and rewriting at home, the first draft of my grant application was ready for Julia's inspection. I had even taken tremendous care to polish up my English, substituting the odd word for something more elegant chosen from my pocket thesaurus. I was reasonably pleased with myself as I entered my office on that Monday morning; even the elevators had conformed to the will of the masses and had actually served to lift me almost to the sixth floor—to be accurate, to the seventh floor. For some reason the elevator refused to stop on the sixth floor, and I was left with the choice of climbing or descending a single set of stairs. Still, it was better than climbing six sets from the ground floor.

After unlocking my office and organizing my desk, I walked down the corridor to see what was going on in my lab. It was after nine a.m. and by then everyone had arrived. I stopped in the hall to chat with Opera-Singh, who was busy preparing a cup of his famous tea. "It is being the only drink that I like," he would re-iterate whenever asked about the vile smell that wafted from his mug. Neal used to joke that when the lab sink frequently became plugged, he would ask Singh for some of his tea and that would flush the drain open immediately. "Opera-Singh's tea, in the sink," Neal would sing off key, "and away go your smelly troubles down the drain... ."

As we were discussing Singh's recent experiments in the hall-way, Neal and Tania came rolling around the corner from the department library and nearly ran us over with the "wheelbar-row." The wheelbarrow was more like a large table with wheels, used primarily to cart supplies and heavy equipment around the department. "Be careful," called out Opera-Singh. "That is being a dangerous enterprise."

Neal braked the wheelbarrow and slowed to a halt with Tania. "What's that?" I asked them.

"These are some of the references for the review," replied Neal evenly. "The average review in that journal has almost two hundred references. We'll start to narrow it down from about six hundred. But we have to decide exactly which way this thing is going."

"We'll sit this afternoon and decide, Neal. In the meantime, don't overdo the reference bit. We do need a lot of good references, but let's settle our exact intentions before doing extra work. You don't want to give yourself and Tania a double hernia, do you?"

"Not at all," agreed Neal, "but it's still better than schizophrenia, manic depressive bipolar disorder, acute paranoia, and all those other fabulous psychoses that we're supposed to be experts on."

"Yes, it certainly is, Neal." What else could I say? I retreated to my office to get some work done. However, I was deeply per-turbed. Why are we all so fascinated by these horrid psychiatric diseases? Are we simply looking for a form of absolution? Is the study of abnormal human behavior an attempt to justify our own faults and failures and to blame genetically inherited faulty biochemical pathways as the major reason for the existence of evil in the world? Is our research not simply absolving us from the need to behave well and from the necessity of justifying the morality of our own behavior? Will rapists and mass murderers in the future point to their own inherited biochemical defects and faulty internal wiring as plausible reasons for their actions? Will we scientists unwillingly, but unavoidably be part of their defense as expert witnesses called to the stand? Suddenly I could envision myself in a future courtroom, trapped by my own scientific research, beneath the volumes of Neal's journals on the wheelbarrow. I could picture one of those slippery lawyers, dressed elegantly in a fancy black suit and tie, with pointy dress shoes on his feet leaning in close for the attack.

"Dr. Miller, you are quoted as saying that acute depression, which has been known to lead to both suicide and homicide, can be caused by a genetic defect, is that correct?"

"Yes, but—"

"Just refrain yourself to answering the question that I ask you, please. Then, Mr. Jones, the accused, may have committed these sixteen serial murders as a result of a decreased or under average level of what you call "Factor Q" in his bloodstream?"

"Well, we have found that levels of Factor Q play a role in depressive—"

"Please, Dr. Miller, just answer the question. It's really quite simple. Could lower than average levels of this Factor Q in Mr. Jones' blood be connected with his depression and subsequent behavior?"

I shook myself out of my reverie and tried to focus on the present. I sat thinking about whether absolution was the real reason for our research. Eventually, I decided that my real quest was to find answers, whichever way they led. I wanted to know what caused these diseases, and once this was known, how they could be prevented or perhaps cured. It's true, such studies might in the long run lead to a simplistic biochemical perception of human behavior, but that might be unavoidable. This seemed to me to be a calculated risk for science. A simplistic, mechanistic molecular view of human behavior and the unfortunate consequences such a misguided philosophy might have on society were necessary evils in our goal of curing horrible behavioral diseases. Throughout history there will always be profiteers, lawyers, and businessmen who capitalize by confiscating certain scientific inventions and discoveries and using them in isolation from their original context. Although scientists are working with the idea of future clinical improvements in the backs of our minds, we have our own hopes and concerns. And mine perhaps had a stopwatch fixed on them more closely than anyone else's. Worse yet, I had no way of knowing how long that stopwatch would give me before the final buzzer would sound. How could I possibly imagine that Grandpa Joe, in one of his usual altruistic attempts, would speed up the sounding of that buzzer?

I barely had time to gather my thoughts together before Neal came charging in through my office door.

"Come in," I said, summoning up all my powers of cynicism. "It's open."

"The bastards!" he exclaimed.

"Don't tell me, the elevators are out of order again," I attempted to chide him.

"It's not funny," he grimaced, beginning to scare me. "I sent Tania to the department darkroom to expose our films from the experiment, and the Smitherians opened up the darkroom door on her and ruined her films!"

Now I was angry, too. "What do you mean, 'they opened the door'? Why didn't she lock it from the inside?"

"She *did* lock it from the inside. In fact, she double locked it. They opened it with a key from the outside. They got impatient waiting for her and to hurry things up began banging on the door. When she calmly continued and was just about to finish, they got tired of waiting and decided to teach her a lesson. They ignored her experiment and just opened the door and ruined everything." Neal was trembling with rage.

I was incredulous. "You're sure they knew that she was in there, and that they didn't think the door was simply locked from the inside with no one in there?"

"Of course they knew she was inside!" Neal shouted. "She answered them when they kept banging on the door and said 'five more minutes'! If you don't solve the problem, I'm going to show them what it's like to mess with us! I'll hook up a remote control light switch to the darkroom and turn it on every time they go in to use the room."

"Okay, okay, calm down. The damage is done. I just want to make sure that the details are correct before I go raise hell with Smithers about this. Calm down. I'll take care of this."

"Whose darkroom is it anyway," Neal muttered, "the department's or Smithers'?"

"That's exactly the point I'm going to raise. But don't worry, we'll settle this, and if necessary, heads will roll. I won't allow such behavior to go on." I had a sudden flash through my head, imagining that the molecular and biochemical basis for mean and egoistic behavior had been discovered, and that it could be treated with little pills, three a day, with almost no side effects. Stop! I must stop imagining these things.

No sooner had I sent Neal back to the lab with assurances that I personally would take care of Smithers and company than the phone rang. I made the mistake of answering it immediately and not waiting to hear who it was on the machine. It was Professor Ernest Stillby.

"Good morning, Dr. Miller." He was always so stiff and formal.

"Good morning, Professor Stillby. How are you?"

Professor Stillby was an almost-retired Professor who worked in the Department of Immunology. He was nearly sixty-five years old, and in recent years his output hadn't been exactly voluminous, to put it bluntly. He was one of those professors who had made his name twenty or twenty-five years ago but had not had the courage and foresight to change with the times. All the methods in biology and biochemistry that are applied in any scientific research today, including his chosen field of immunology, had changed immensely over the past ten years—not to mention the past twenty. Moreover, no scientist who respected himself could possibly ignore the revolution posed by the introduction of molecular biology methods. These new molecular methods, as opposed to the more traditional "cellular" methods, depended far less on the observation of whole cells in the microscope. The molecular methods allowed researchers to probe deep within the cell itself to examine specific DNA and levels of RNA and protein in the cells under a variety of physiological conditions, thus allowing an assessment of the "lifestyle" of the cells. Today's science without these newer molecular methods greatly restricted the ability of the scientist to progress; it was like an accountant without a computer or even a calculator. It was analogous to the practice of medicine where there were only general practitioners available; any patient needing cardiac surgery, psychiatric evaluation, or bone setting would find himself lacking the proper treatment. I knew that it was very hard for some of the older professors to undergo this transition. No lab could turn overnight into a totally new environment. However, most of the more determined older professors still managed to understand the newer techniques. In most cases they needed to form partnerships with some of the younger labs in order to incorporate them into their own systems, but that was generally not a problem. Where there's a will, there's a way. Some of the older professors found younger postdocs to come in and work for them for a few years and introduce these new methods to their technicians and younger students. Unfortunately for Professor Stillby, as some of the psychologists might note, he stayed fixed in the oral stage or anal stage or whatever. But all that was his problem; my problem was that he was also probably sitting on the committee for my tenure. I couldn't help thinking that with his pomposity, my tenure could actually be decided by something ridiculous, like whether he thinks I'm polite enough to him.

Professor Stillby spoke into the telephone, "Fine thank you. It's very hard to get hold of you, did you know?"

He spoke extremely slowly, as if biting down and clamping his teeth on each word. In fact, his style of speaking reminded me slightly of good old Micky-fucking-Morooney from my high school days, but without the obscenities, obviously.

"Yes, I can imagine."

"By the way," he noted casually, "there's a young man who answered the phone a few times in your lab. Extremely rude. No patience at all. It's very disrespectful, especially when I've mentioned that it's me that he's speaking to."

129

The arrogant, pompous old fool, I thought to myself. Why couldn't Tania have answered the phone? I could understand Neal losing his patience with Stillby, but I had enough troubles right now without having to make an issue out of it. I calmed the old professor down, explaining that things were still very hectic in the lab, and requested pleasantly that he leave messages on my office machine or even at home. Unfortunately, he could only be partially placated. After finally scheduling a meeting with me to discuss some of the recent results of one of his students, he returned to the topic of Neal and insisted that I give the rude young man a decent "talking to." In his day, it had probably been a decent "thrashing," but those good old days were gone now. I had no choice but to agree.

Then, I gathered my courage together and walked over to Smithers' office. After the rather cool greetings, I went in and closed the door behind me. I said rather brashly, "Tell me, Lewis, do you realize how much time and money your gang cost me this morning?" I was careful to allocate the damage to myself and not to Tania or Neal. Direct damage done to me was obviously far more serious for someone like Smithers.

Lewis Smithers was a short, thin balding man with steel-rimmed glasses that hid his shrewd brown eyes. His stringy, greasy black hair was carefully grown long on the side of his head where the hair still grew and combed deceitfully across his balding mid-skull. Needless to say, Smithers disliked windy weather, which endangered the maintenance of his rather complex hairstyle, and he forbade his students to open the lab windows on the pretext of maintaining "sterile conditions." This morning, he sat back in what Neal called his "president's chair" and smiled grimly. "I heard only rumors of a small skirmish this morning. But my group says that your people are in there, sometimes for hours at a time."

I thought fervently, trying to find the best way to relate to his untrue claims. I said evenly, "You know, nobody spends *hours* in the darkroom. But if every time someone who is unhappy at the length of someone else's experiment decides to open the door, there'll be chaos. Aside from ruining two weeks of work," I exaggerated, "a whole set of new films were exposed and ruined. Either I get an apology from your students, with a promise that they never do such a thing again, or I go to Nussensweig with a complaint. This darkroom belongs to the department, and your students will not decide what type of experiments we do, what is too large and what is too long. You're the boss; you decide," I stormed.

"Well, yes. There's no need to drag Nussensweig in. I'll have my people apologize. But can't you try to spend less time in the darkroom?"

I was adamant, "Look, it's not a question of time in the darkroom. My students don't go in there to meditate or play tennis. If they need the time to expose and develop films in there, then they need the time. Have you been in there recently? It's hot enough to fry eggs on the bench. There's no air—it's not a place for a picnic! No one spends more time than they need to in there. I'm warning you, I will not allow your students to intimidate mine. I swear to you that if anything like this ever occurs again, I guarantee that whoever is responsible is out of this department. It's antiscientific and antihumanitarian."

"Alright, no need to get so upset. I'll have a word with them. Let's keep it between us. No need to get the head of the department involved in these silly affairs."

What a relief that Nussensweig is such a fair and impartial man, I thought to myself. Smithers is actually afraid of him. Before heading back to the lab, I decided to call Julia and ask her to meet me for lunch. I would spring the draft of the grant on her.

"I'm really glad you called," she said. "I had wanted to call myself, but didn't want to pressure you with the grant. I feel badly that you're doing most of the hard work."

"Not at all," I replied cheerfully. "In fact, that's part of the reason why I'm calling. The first draft is ready for your inspection and hopefully your approval too."

"So that's the only reason why you want to meet me for lunch," she chided me.

"No, of course not, but it's good to have a professional reason to fall back on. That way, I'm less likely to show my disappointment if you show a lack of interest in such a meeting."

"Well, you have my permission to invite me to lunch or whatever," she said somewhat mysteriously, "for nonprofessional reasons, if you have them."

"Great," I said. "Then 12:45 for a professional lunch with the possibility of extending or modifying the invitation to nonprofessional terms?"

"See you there," she agreed and we hung up.

Within the hour, Dr. Julia Kearns and I were facing off down at the cafeteria, with our trays of vile-smelling lunch before us. Even Julia made a face at her tray this time, no longer pretending that the food was particularly appetizing. "I won't even tell you about Neal's theories concerning this cafeteria. That would completely mess up our lunch," I joked with her.

I was in a good mood despite the little feuds I had had to settle that morning. I wanted to discuss business first with Julia and then perhaps gather up the courage to ask her out to dinner one evening. I was still debating whether I should wait until she read the draft and gave me her criticisms, but I was beginning to feel that the time was becoming ripe. Duffy was already an almost surrealistic memory, and I had managed to avoid both Jim's and Carol's phone calls that weekend. I also knew that sometimes the commencement of these things had their own rhythm that could not be altered. If I delayed now, it might be too late. Julia had already hinted on the phone that she would be willing to go out with me. What more did I need? Even a delay of two weeks might prove to be crucial. Proper timing was often essential in starting a new relationship, and even if I had had other plans, disregarding such positive signs was a definite risk.

We discussed our grant application, and Julia promised to read it within a few days and to get back to me immediately afterwards. The conversation slowly drifted away from the grant, and looking at her, with her fine posture and pretty features, I asked her, "Julia, may I ask you two personal questions?"

"Sure," she answered easily.

"The first one is easier for me to ask, so you can treat it like a warm-up question: Why did you choose psychiatry as your specialty?"

Julia looked at me evenly, speaking with that clear, candid voice of hers, "That's a question I often ask myself. The answer, I suppose, as we psychiatrists tend to say, is complex and stems from a number of reasons. To begin with, I have always been interested in the balance between physiology and psychology, and psychiatry deals with the chemical aspects of this balance. In addition, as opposed to most doctors, I always found it very difficult to get used to blood. That narrowed down greatly the number of specialties I could choose, since practically every specialty has its need for surgery. I should also mention that the professor who taught psychiatry back then was excellent and attracted many residents to the field. But I think that I'd be skirting the truth if I didn't mention that my mother's brother, my Uncle James, had schizophrenia. Ever since I was young, I have been struggling to understand the manifestations of that and other psychiatric illnesses."

I looked at her with understanding, feeling very close, with tears almost coming to my eyes. "I know exactly what you mean."

Julia looked at me in what I imagined and perhaps hoped was a compassionate manner.

"Do you have similar reasons for choosing this area of research yourself?" she asked gently.

"My father suffers from bipolar disorder. There's nothing I would want more than to learn something that could help him. It's become practically an obsession."

"I understand," replied Julia. "It must be harder for those of you who work exclusively in research. I can be comforted by helping other people who are ill. It's a form of absolution. But you are not content until you enhance understanding of the illness.

That's the curiosity that you researchers are endowed with."

"Absolution," I pondered, "funny you should say that." I took a sip from my juice and tried to gently change the subject. "Regarding the other personal question?"

"Shoot," she answered.

"Would you like to go out for a nonprofessional meal at a real restaurant one evening, a place where the food is actually edible?" The words came out quickly, as though someone had shot them out of my mouth like a hockey puck. I was afraid of turning back at this point. I had to go forward.

"I'd like that very much," she answered, to my combined relief, surprise, and happiness.

CHAPTER ELEVEN

I returned to my office in a state of euphoria, happier than I had been in some time. I didn't even mind climbing up the six flights of stairs, with both elevators temporarily out of order again. Perhaps it would be fairer to say that the elevators were temporarily *in order* on those rare occasions when they were actually working. I was celebrating two massive victories with myself. Not only had Julia agreed and actually voiced interest in going out with me, but I had finally broken the blood brain barrier or BBB, as we neurologists say, and found the courage to ask her. The BBB serves as a natural dam to prevent the penetration of unwanted cells and various other large particles from getting into the brain. I felt that since my separation from Jeannie, I had formed a sort of homemade "psychological BBB," preventing me from starting new relationships—real emotional ones and not just sexual outlets. After the disintegration of my marriage with Jeannie, dismantling my own BBB was no simple matter. Aside from the numerous unsuccessful matchmaking attempts by Carol and Jim, the last of which seemed to culminate in Duffy's wide bed, I found myself absolutely paralyzed in the realm of courting women. I felt that I just didn't have it in me. I lacked the patience for those clever phone calls and the light banter of conversation and the tenacity to send flowers day after day. I feared the long conversations necessary to get to know someone new and the possibility that after so much time invested together, there would be incompatibilities. I would poke into the future right from the start, peeking behind the ritual courtship games to foresee possible disagreements, arguments, and strife that lay in ambush just around the corner. Will she accept Compo? How will she react when I tell her what my childhood was like and how my relationship is with my family today? Will she let me sleep on the side of the bed that I like? Will she chew gum, which I cannot stand? Does she have faith in any religious denomination? Could I live with that? Will she accept the long hours I put into my career? Something within me was deeply pessimistic and had no time for the lightness and the sweetness. The lightness blinded me; I needed sunglasses. As for the sweetness, it tasted like cough syrup. It was as though I wanted a stable relationship right from the start, with all the ground rules set up. Like a Chinese food take-away dinner with four full courses, all set to go. My being would cry out and say: I'm really like this, or at least I will be once you get to know me. Take it or leave it. Most left it. Or, if they did take it, they soon left it within a few short years, as Jeannie did. I was not an easy person to get along with. I knew that. Jeannie knew that. Jim and Carol also knew that. Even Compo could certainly vouch for that. Jim once summed up my behavior some time after my separation from Jeannie by saying that I didn't know how to take things day by day, as they came. He claimed that no sooner had I gained any new knowledge or information than my mind was already analytically calculating the eventual consequences and subtle meanings of that knowledge—grinding out all the intricate possibilities and desperately racing to figure out all the permutations and combinations. I always answered Jim by saying that he took life far too passively, and that there were many things he could mold and shape, if not entirely change, by thinking things out in advance, like me. I maintained that with proper planning and preparation, Jim could better control his life.

"Man," Jim would shake his head with disbelief, "that may be true, but look at the toll these calculations take on you. You spend so much time preoccupied with these thoughts, ninety-nine percent of which are absolutely hypothetical, that you don't have time left to smell the flowers on the way."

"But Jim, at least I get to the garden. You don't necessarily find your way to the garden, never mind the flowers."

"That's the difference between us, Steve. I don't care all that much whether I get to the garden or not, but I enjoy the way, whichever direction it leads. Sometimes I get to a citrus orchard in the spring, and sometimes I end up at a busy traffic inter-section. It doesn't matter, either way I look at the positive side of things wherever I am. Though orange trees smell great when they bloom in the spring, there are also many beautiful cars that drive by at a busy intersection, filled with the newest technol-ogy. But you," he said pointing his finger at me accusingly, "if you arrive at a park instead of a garden, you raise hell until you redirect yourself. Loosen up. You won't turn into a carefree hobo. You don't have to worry about that! But think a little about what I said!"

Jim would probably be surprised to know that I thought a lot about what he said; rarely a day went by when I didn't find my-self wondering what it would be like to be more carefree and less planned and programmed. Would I be happier with less stress and anxiety? Or would I feel deserted, left with the empty shells of already-fired adrenaline that no longer surged through my system? Did my own genetic makeup even allow me the option of Jim's type of lifestyle? The answer to these questions, I suspected, as Dr. Julia Kearns would say, is complex and not clear cut.

I walked over to the department library to pour myself a much needed cup of coffee. Neal was there with his wheelbarrow, still digging into potential references for the review article. He had three timers pinned to his lab coat and was fervently marking bound volumes to be photocopied.

"Busy day, Neal?" I inquired with a touch of sarcasm. Neal didn't notice my sarcastic attitude or at least he chose to ignore it.

"No, I've got time today, so I really want to start on the review and get my teeth sunk into it." He had a mechanical pencil placed horizontally above his right ear and he looked, from where I was standing, like a carpenter's apprentice. Only the tattered carpenter's overalls were replaced by his tattered jeans. Then he leaned over in what I assumed was a conspiratorial manner and whispered, "Are you alright, Steve?"

"Sure," I replied, puzzled by his concern. I was already trying to analyze whether my happiness with today's turn of events could be read so easily on my forehead, even by someone like Neal. That wasn't really a fair thought. I knew that beneath Neal's somewhat abrasive and seemingly impenetrable exterior lay a very sensitive young man. Neal did not relish exposing any part of himself that could even vaguely be attributed as a weakness. For this reason, he was very, very cautious about sharing that side of him with anyone he didn't trust.

He leaned on the wheelbarrow and his penetrating eyes glared at me with a curious, respectful type of stare. He edged towards me cautiously, running his hand over the short stubble of hair on his egg-shaped head and whispered again, "Whatever did you say to Smithers? He locked up his cult here in the library for two hours this morning and Ken says that the walls were shaking. Six point something on the Richter scale. Does that have anything to do with the darkroom?"

Since my exhilarating lunch with Julia, my thoughts and concerns about the problems in the department really had escaped my attentions. My confrontation with Smithers and all the other politics that I had dealt with only hours ago now seemed like historical feuds. Neal's question really jolted me out of my euphoria. I looked at him quizzically at first and then quickly regained my countenance. "You bet, Neal. Don't ever say that I don't back you up when you've got troubles here in the lab. Just do your work, and I'll take care of Smithers and his harem when necessary."

At the mention of the word "harem," Neal smirked. It was true that for some reason Smithers had collected mostly female students. I hadn't meant to be disrespectful or to delegitimize Smithers' chosen students; I had merely intended to point out a fact. I quickly said, "Neal, I hope you won't spread that comment—"

Neal abruptly cut into my flow of words while simultaneously making an extended motion with his arms as if to verify what his mouth was saying, "Don't worry, I won't quote your 'harem' phrase to anyone else. If I use it, I'll quote myself. But it's quite accurate, really, the way they suck up to him."

"Come on, Neal," I argued, almost not noticing that we had now switched sides in the discussion. Like a planned debate, we had reverted 180 degrees. "Don't exaggerate. What goes on over there isn't all *that* bad."

"No?!" raved Neal. "Did you know that they have a fully active 'Smitherian intelligence system' set up? Gina faxed John le Carré for advice on how to get a mole—not the gram-over-molecular weight type—into Smithers' midst. They know exactly which Saturdays Smithers plans to come and work here in his office, and only on those weekends do they bother to come and work. Have you noticed that as soon as he goes home in the evening, his lab empties within ten minutes? Smithers' students are obviously extremely clever; I can't even fathom how they work out their experiments like that. Imagine if you said to me that you're going home soon, say at four o'clock. My polyacrylamide gel with the protein samples will only finish its run by about 5:45, whether I like it or not. So how do they manage? Do they throw away experiments when Smithers goes home early, or what? And what about when he goes abroad to meetings? Is anyone ever working here after five o'clock? They probably employ a satellite to keep up with the intelligence. If you're interested, we could probably get an accurate weather report out of them! Blizzard warning coming from Alberta and the west."

"Okay, Neal, you've made your point. Still, I'd be most grateful if you'd keep that 'harem' statement to yourself. I don't want to get the feminists angry."

139

"No problem, no problem, don't worry."

I stirred my coffee and walked back to my office. I knew that with Neal, I didn't have to worry. He always did what he said. Sometimes he even paid a tremendous price to keep his word, too. That was his nature. I recalled my first encounter with Neal, about four years ago, when I interviewed him as a candidate Ph.D. student. Neal came from a small farming town just outside of Edmonton. He didn't get along very well with his parents and most of his six brothers and sisters and was looked at by his family as an oddball. Being the oldest of the Parsons children, Neal's father had had great expectations. He didn't hope to sire a Nobel prize–winning scientist, or even a Ph.D. graduate for that matter, but intended for Neal to eventually take over the Alberta farm. Apparently, Neal's parents had been extremely surprised and upset by his sudden decision to seek higher education in Edmonton after barely scraping through his local high school. Neal had always been a workhorse on the farm, an asset to his entire family. In addition to working with the combines, harvesters, tractors, and plows, he had golden hands. He mastered carpentry and metalworks and even taught himself rudimentary welding skills. In the lab, Neal was invaluable; he built shelves and stands for equipment, including our computers, and was a wizard with electrical connections. He would even clean my carburetor now and then in the parking lot when the weather was nice, claiming that the noise drove him mad. It didn't sound any different to my untrained ears, even after Neal's tune-ups, but I never did have any trouble with my carburetor.

Every now and then, I would kid him about his "pitchfork days" or tease him about how soft his hands had become. Aside from one or two long conversations, Neal spoke very little of his family, except for one married sister who now lived in Toronto. Despite his multiple talents, he had skidded through high school hating it intensely. That's not surprising, because everything was intense with Neal. He seemed to divide his likes and dislikes to distinct compartments, with very precise decisions regarding the selection process. There was a black department and a white one, but no gray category. There were not even areas of gradation around the black or white or changes in the light. Neal either trusted someone or he didn't. On several occasions Neal told me accounts of his high school days. Apparently, he spent nearly as much time in Jasper and the Rockies as he did in school. I imagined that Neal had been bored by school and inattentive, with his potential wholly untapped. He arrived here in Toronto like a maple tree brimmed to the top with sap, just bursting with all that potential syrup inside of him. I knew that Neal had gone on to the university in Edmonton and had done both his bachelor's and master's degrees there. When I interviewed him, his documents practically said it all: top grades and a superb master's record, including the publication of an article that he had brought with him as proof of his scientific credibility. However, the clincher was his letter of recommendation from his master's supervisor, Professor Jensen. The letter said that not only was Neal very bright and capable, but that his most powerful attribute was his motivation. It was worded as follows: "Being a military man myself, I'll use the following analogy. Neal not only has the motivation, drive, and willpower of an army officer, he has the motivation, drive, and willpower of an entire platoon of generals. He might even be the next NATO commander of science. This young man has a potentially exciting future ahead of him."

Despite these credentials, when Smithers saw me interview Neal as my first real candidate Ph.D. student, he took me aside and offered his unwanted opinion. He strongly advised me against accepting Neal. "That young man looks terribly unstable. I wouldn't trust those hicks from out west," he said to me in that typical demeaning manner of his. To this day, I wonder whether Smithers was aware of my own hometown and intended to hurt me. After all, Regina isn't too much farther east than Edmonton. I find it hard to believe that he forgot that I was from Saskatchewan. Smithers never forgot much; it was far more likely that the comment was intended as one of his rather crude insults.

That was his style and it came in addition to his own warped and ill-informed opinion of Neal's abilities. At the time I was too astonished and naïve to even repeal his attack. I just listened and let his advice roll in one ear and out the other. Today, I wouldn't stand for such behavior from him. There were two possibilities for this brutal attack. One was that his snobbery towards western Canada was so great that he really had no regard for the citizens of those provinces. After all, he himself was born and raised in Toronto, as he would proudly announce at every opportunity available. The other possibility was that he was envious and angry that Neal hadn't even gone to speak to him about possibly doing his Ph.D. in *his* lab. Neal had been interviewed by several other lab directors, one of them was also based in this department, but he had not even bothered to talk to Smithers. What nerve, to choose *me* over Smithers! Worse yet, to prove to be more worthy than Smithers' own lot! An abomination!

Neal was clearly beginning to develop some new skills. He had been demonstrating his capabilities in thinking, devising, and executing quality research for several years now in my lab and for two years prior to that back in Edmonton. He was blessed with that unusual foresight where he intuitively knew how to choose the simplest, most direct, and promising approaches to address scientific problems. Many times over the years Neal and I would spend hours trying to decide the best way to tackle a certain problem. Neal would argue vehemently in favor of a certain approach, while I often objected, claiming that a different method was more advisable. To Neal's credit, not only did he usually win those fierce arguments, but his way of experimentation was inevitably fruitful. Aside from exhibiting wisdom in his choice of experimental approach, he also had a very soft touch in the actual execution. Many of the new methods had to be calibrated prior to adapting them to our own utilization, but somehow Neal's studies almost always provided results. In research, even a success rate of ten to twenty percent for experiments is considered good. Frequently we scientists face problems more complex than whether the experiment actually succeeds, such as if it provides *any* information at all. Neal's work almost inevitably provided informative results.

At this point he was beginning to assume a new level of confidence. He was teaching Tania and Ken. He was showing sparks of leadership and organizational abilities that were rare, given that he had been blessed with so many other talents. Even his communication skills seemed to be improving. There was no need to improve his efficiency or time-management skills, and it was definitely unnecessary for him to increase his level of awareness so that people wouldn't take advantage of him. No one was going to take advantage of Neal. Of *that* I was absolutely certain. Neal had antennae as wide as a football field for sensing any intentions to take advantage of him.

I began to focus on my work for the day and to prepare my outline for my part of the course that Smithers and I were teaching together, Molecular and Cell Biology of Neurological and Psychiatric Disorders. Smithers, of course, concentrated on the neurological disorders, his area of specialization, teaching students about such horrible illnesses as Alzheimer's and the fascinating and imminently strange rediscovered mad cow disease and Creutzfeld–Jakob disease, its accompanying human manifestation. He also taught sections about Parkinson's disease and several other neurological disorders. Smithers' curriculum also included teaching a general section dealing with techniques in molecular biology to be used as tools in developing new diagnostic methods. To his credit, Smithers was a good lecturer, preparing his course with much forethought and demanding much from the students. There were occasional complaints that surfaced at the medical school administrative offices concerning Smithers' unrefined manner in dealing with the students and their questions. However, most of the students grudgingly admitted that he was one of the better teachers in the medical school and the entire institute. I taught the other half of the course, dealing with topics that Smithers didn't particularly favor. The topics of my lectures included discussions concerning the molecular mechanisms that regulate psychiatric disorders, among them depressions of various types, bipolar disorder, psychotic behaviors such as schizophrenia, and others. In addition to trying to raise interest in the study of these diseases, one of my important goals was to teach the young scientists and medical students that many of these diseases, despite their "psychiatric" denomination, have physiological explanations, some more simple and others more complex. Moreover, my intention was to make the students understand that even those psychiatric illnesses whose physiological or molecular basis has not yet been comprehensively characterized still held a reasonable chance of being understood in several years' time. That, of course, depends on whether researchers in the field are successful and manage to persuade enough talented, younger investigators to pursue these venues of research. Unfortunately, many older and more established researchers, such as Smithers, hold a very dim view of our work and its significance. Smithers, despite being an extremely clever scientist, cannot break away from the preconceptions associated with psychiatric disease. He still hasn't grasped that psychiatric diseases should be treated much as neurological illnesses and researched in the same fashion. In fact, years ago, in a rare attempt at collegial friendship, he suggested quite seriously: "Leave that sinking ship and try real research. You've got to put *'matter over mind.'*" This was one of those rare instances where each of us interpreted that phrase in a wholly different way. It was hard for me to be angry with him for *that*. For once he was actually trying to be comradely and truly make a suggestion that he perceived was in my best interests. However, needless to say, I rejected his advice politely. Even regarding our course, Smithers was always trying to give me the feeling that he was only doing me a favor by teaching the course together with me. He found my choice of lecture topics to be insignificant. He only agreed to teach the course together with me because we were in the same department. Several times a year I would threaten to teach my own course without him, leaving him to prepare a whole new section and to deliver an entire course on his own. Apparently, the excessive amount of work that he would have if he chose that particular option made him rethink the idea each time anew. I would have been perfectly satisfied to teach my own course without Smithers' neurological section. From my understanding, the attendance would not have dropped much. Although Smithers was highly respected as a lecturer, I got the feeling that most of the students really chose this course option to learn a subject about which they had previously heard very little: the physiological and nonphysiological aspects of behavioral disorders. There were even psychology students and qualified psychologists who asked me for permission to attend my section of the course, apparently hoping to broaden their understanding. In fact, I was just waiting for Smithers to bow out and leave me the whole course. I could then add sections about the hunt for the genes involved in schizophrenia and bipolar disorder in afflicted families with high rates of intermarriage, such as the Amish. I even speculated on the addition of a lecture or two on anxiety disorders, known as GADs (generalized anxiety disorders) and recent findings of a gene that predisposes people to these afflictions.

I soon had to steel myself for my annual confrontation with Smithers regarding the course examination. Every year, he would insist on making up a multiple choice exam that greatly facilitated the grading of the course. I firmly objected. I believed that this course, including Smithers' lectures, was supposed to do two things in general. First of all, it aimed to teach the students the basic biology and underlying mechanisms responsible for various neurological and psychiatric diseases. Second, I wanted the course to provide the students with the tools to develop deductive abilities and the potential to critically examine scientific research in general. I was in favor of preparing an exam where it could be determined whether these goals had been achieved, even at the cost of correcting and grading somewhat longer answers that allowed the students to rationalize and justify their answers. For the past four years, I had ultimately been able to convince Smithers to adopt my style of exam. I hoped that this year would be no different.

My mind drifted to the course, and I found myself pulling out a calendar to see exactly when my teaching was scheduled to begin. With the calendar open, my mind made another quantum leap and hopped back to the next orbital shelf to see the date of my planned meeting with Julia. I felt like a sixteen year old, unable to wait for the day to finally arrive. What would I do with myself until then? Then the real question crept up on me from behind: What would I do *after* the date?

CHAPTER TWELVE

My curriculum vitae and life history of going out with members of the opposite sex dated back about twenty-one or twenty-two years. We seekers of tenure remain firmly fixed with the obsessive confines of our limited scientific-academic jargon. Even reminiscing induces us to summon such terms as "curriculum vitae" and "publication list," as well as those clinchers like "grant," "references," "abstract," and "committee." We live in a world of our own, in a voluntary manner often totally secluded and protected from the "real world." We have our own concerns—raising funds for research, publishing papers, national and international competition, and the struggle for recognition. People from the outside often find it difficult to understand our obsessions with this private little world. My British mate, Nigel, who has been living in Toronto now for many years, never fails to note, "I say, Steve, if you'd put half that much energy into some business, any bloody business, you'd be a jolly wealthy man right now."

However unstable my state of wealth or tenure right now, it did not prevent me from sliding back along the arrow of time to recall my very first date in high school. At about that period, my family had returned to our Wascana Drive haven, albeit without mom. Grandpa Joe had moved in to live with us full time, but since I was already sixteen and Ervin was thirteen and increasingly independent, only Cindy was really in need of a "mother" around the home. The real reason that Grandpa Joe came to live with us was obviously to take care of dad. But that wasn't the official reason that Grandpa Joe gave; for all his help, support, and goodwill, he could never admit that his own son was more or less permanently ill and could not function as a parent to his own offspring.

"I vant to keep an eye on Ervin," he would whisper to me on more than one occasion, "to make sure he grows up to be a 'mensch.'"

I often wondered if mensch, the Yiddish word for a well-behaved man, meant for Grandpa Joe that Ervin would never vote for a socialist party when he grew up. To Ervin, at other times he would say, "It's good that I stay here ven Steve is under so much stress; vait until you get to high school and see how much vork there is."

To Cindy, Grandpa Joe wouldn't bother explaining. She was now almost twelve years old, and the reason for Grandpa Joe's decision to live with us was not exactly an issue that rated high on her mind. She didn't bother dwelling on the precise reasons but took the situation as it was.

Times were rough in those years. We children did not have much actual time to see mom during the week; it was far too hectic on a regular basis. First of all, mom still worked long hard hours both at the hospital and in her private ENT clinic. I now realize that she was still struggling to pay off some of the heavy bank loans she had received to help repurchase our home. Then, on those few evenings when mom finished her work at a reasonable hour, it would still be late by the time that she drove across the city from her apartment to meet us. She and Paul lived way at the other end of the city, and even in the absence of traffic, the drive still took twenty-five to thirty minutes. However, the major problem was that once mom arrived, she would have no choice but to take us out of the house. Dad went into an absolutely terrible emotional state that bordered on violence even at the very mention of mom's name. Dad's ego had been hurt badly by mom's "abandoning" him. As difficult as it is for a mentally healthy person to suffer a marital breakup, this was something incomprehensible and catastrophic for someone in dad's state. Dad's extreme reaction was not wholly unexpected. To make matters worse, for all his cleverness and stability, Grandpa Joe sided with dad in this case and would not allow mom to set foot in the house. No amount of persuasion, logic, or candid conversation could sway Grandpa Joe in this matter. "Does a captain leave a sinking ship? Vat kind of marriage breaks up because someone is temporarily sick. Vat about the marriage vows, 'for better or for vorse'?"

So to see us during the week mom would have to cross the city four times: once to come and pick us up, once to take us over to her shared flat with Paul, once to bring us home at the end of the evening, and once, of course, to drive herself back home. This routine was no easy task, especially in the extreme, frigid, Regina winters. Despite the severe inconvenience involved, mom would still try to do this at least once or twice a week. By now she had altogether given up any hope of maintaining a working relationship with Grandpa Joe—never mind with dad.

Our real opportunity to be with mom was on the weekends. The summers were the best, because Paul owned a small but pleasant log cabin on the shore of Witkona Lake, a little star-shaped lake surrounded by forests just outside Regina. Paul and mom would take us all out for the weekend to the lake. As opposed to some of the better-known Saskatchewan lakes, Witkona Lake's main attraction was its tranquility. There were no real towns or neighborhoods or streets—just a few scattered cabins, with poor access via dirt roads. The cabins themselves generally had minimal luxuries, such as running water, but no televisions and dishwashers. The lovely woods encompassing the lake were bursting in season with blueberries, raspberries, and mushrooms, and mom and Paul would walk for hours around the lake. Upon arrival, Ervin would spend hours digging for worms and paddling about near Paul's dock in an inflatable plastic dinghy angling for fish. Rarely did he ever catch anything, but the time away from dad and the refreshing nature out at the lake had a calming effect on him. One Saturday morning out at the lake, Ervin came running up the path to the cabin, yelling and shouting, all excited with himself, "I caught something! Come quick! Come see!"

Mom and I followed Paul down to the dock, where Ervin had left his fishing rod with a fair-sized northern pike hooked to the end. The poor fish was struggling hard to extricate itself from the hook, bouncing up and down erratically on the dock, but the line was too short and the pike had no way of reaching the water. I caught mom grimacing as she inspected the predicament of the fish, and I couldn't help wondering whether she was thinking of something more personal than the fish. The memory of mom's shocked expression stayed frozen like a slide in my brain for many years. Recently, I tried to ask her if she remembered what she had been thinking of when she first viewed Ervin's poor fish, but she didn't even remember the situation. So many times I have gone through my own life, imagining other people's thoughts and feelings when they encounter certain events—events that seem to have a serious impact. Sometimes, as in this particular case, I was sure that the situation meant a great deal to mom, and that it would not be easily forgotten. In most cases, I have been dead wrong. Perhaps my suppositions and baseless assumptions have managed to get me into much trouble in my own private life. This seems especially true in my short marriage with Jeannie and in other relationships with women. Fortunately for me, in my scientific work I avoid relying on such dangerous instinct.

Paul saved the day by skillfully removing Ervin's fish from the hook and putting a quick end to its suffering. He eventually cleaned and cooked it for Ervin for dinner. It wasn't big enough to provide a meal for us all, but Ervin proudly insisted that everyone taste his fish. He was badly in need of excelling at something and was glad for the recognition that his fishing had brought him.

That winter I turned seventeen. Fortunately, I had moved to a new high school. This school prided itself on catering to its more motivated students by designing a unique program where the level of the curriculum was supposedly higher. I didn't really notice any particular difference either in the level of the courses themselves or in the teaching, but the students who were enrolled in this program were very different from those with whom I had become accustomed. There were no Ricks or Micky Morooneys in the classroom, and that, to me, was far more important than the level of the classes. I was still unpopular, but no longer despised and ridiculed. That was a great improvement. At this time, the major barrier between my popularity and unpopularity appeared to reside with me. I was rather unsociable and didn't make friends easily. However, I didn't really care. The main thing was that I wasn't making enemies; particularly the type that like to give out chocolate whirlies.

Part of my dilemma stemmed from the wretched situation at home. I felt that I couldn't comfortably invite friends over to visit me at the house, which would eventually create immense problems, leaving me exposed to ridicule. I was afraid to make new friends, go out and visit with them, and do all those activities that high school friends normally do together. My fear was that eventually I would be forced to invite them to my house. I couldn't cope with the thought that they would see dad and how Grandpa Joe was caring for him. I preferred to remain anonymous, alone but without enemies rather than being ridiculed for my unusually weird and dysfunctional family.

One afternoon in physics class, Mr. Fowler was returning tests that we had written in our previous class. The test was on mechanics and waves, if I'm not mistaken, and he praised two of us who both received 100% on the exam: Steve Miller and Jim Wilson. Immediately after the class, Jim came over to my desk to congratulate me. "Nice going, Steve. He's not a bad teacher, is he?"

Jim was a tall young man, with narrow shoulders and boyish good looks. He also had a rather serious expression on his face, which was somewhat unusual among teenagers, even those enrolled in "the program" as it was known at the school. I answered evenly, "He's not bad at all. You should see some of the science teachers at Wilmer Heights, where I was last year."

Jim whistled. "You went to Wilmer Heights? Did you just move into the neighborhood here? Did you live in Wilmer Heights before?"

Before I knew it, Jim and I were skating together at the outdoor rink near our homes. It turned out that Jim lived not too far away, in an apartment complex with his younger brother and mother. Jim had also had a tragic childhood. When he was only five years old, his father had been shot and killed. Mr. Wilson had died trying to prevent an armed robber from running off with all the money in the cash register of their small family delicatessen. Next to Jim, I suddenly felt that I was not the only one in the world who had problems to overcome. We became very close friends, and I confided in him, explaining my own family situation. Jim was not repulsed; he often came over for dinner and enjoyed bantering with Grandpa Joe, engaging him in conversations about the recent Saskatchewan elections and teasing him about the rise of the labor party. He also loved Grandpa Joe's "old style" Jewish food and would spend hours trying to persuade him to make up another batch of his famous knishes, chicken soup, pierogies, and gefilte fish. "You clean the mess ven I finish with the dough and I make a batch of knishes," Grandpa Joe would say.

"Deal," Jim would confirm, elated. This type of food would remind him of the days when his own father had been alive. An old Jewish woman had once cooked and baked for the delicatessen, and Jim had developed his refined taste for Jewish food at an early age.

Surprisingly, Jim was not afraid of dad. Neither his moods nor the closed doors seemed to affect him. In fact, Jim was a social, old-style gentleman, with such a good disposition that he seemed to have a calming effect on dad. Many a time, although barricaded in his room, dad would invite Jim in to talk. Mom's psychological babble would maintain that Jim was looking for a father figure, but I just think that Jim had such an easy manner that it was difficult for anyone not to get along with him. He was always willing to help out. More than once, I can recall Jim managing to convince dad to come out of his room, have dinner with us all, and even play Scrabble or watch a hockey game on television. That's not to say that dad didn't occasionally come out of his shell even when Jim wasn't around, but Jim's presence definitely had a stabilizing effect on him. Perhaps dad, whose own father was so important to him, felt that Jim also needed a father figure. But that was mom's theory. Regardless of the reasoning, my friendship with Jim was a trigger to many improvements both inside and outside the house.

Through my association with Jim, I suddenly found that I had a new social life. It wasn't much, but compared with what it had been before and given my own unwillingness to invest in it, it was still something. I found myself going out with Jim to Friday night parties. These outings were not my "bag of fun"; I preferred being alone with Jim or having him over at my place. I didn't like to share him with all the others at the party. But I felt that I had to go to those parties. First of all, it was better than staying home. Second, I was afraid that Jim would lose interest in me or fear that his own social status would be jeopardized by his friendship with such a social reject who wouldn't even go to parties.

There wasn't much for me to do at these parties, except wait until they ended. They gave me a chance to meditate and reflect on many things. The partygoers seemed to be divided more or less into two groups, with some overlap between them; one group was the dancers. They would be bouncing and thrashing around happily to the heavy beat of the ear-wrenching music. The second group was the drinkers. A bottle of Johnny Walker would be passed around from mouth to mouth. The drinkers were generally a quieter group, mostly withdrawn into themselves. Some passed out in the darker corners of the basements where these parties usually took place. I found it easiest to mimic the latter less active and less communicative group, but I didn't need the alcohol for my own introspection. I sat and stared fixedly at the ceiling for hours, wondering if I would ever meet some girl who thought like I did. Jim would breeze by now and then, sweating profusely from the dancing and say things like, "Great party, eh?" I would try my best to beam back my "approval," but Jim would be back on the dance floor, bouncing away like on a trampoline.

One winter afternoon, I was walking home from school with Jim when he asked me, "Steve, would you like to come with Robyn and me on a double date on Friday?"

I looked down at the crispy snow underfoot and then looked into Jim's eyes. "Come on Jim, you know I couldn't find anyone to go with."

"No, seriously, Steve. I'll find someone you'll get along with. Come on, it'll be fun. What about Pamela Turner?"

"I don't even know her, Jim. You're better off on your own. Besides, as popular as you may be, I don't think that Pam will be likely to agree to go out with me. And I don't want you to lie to anyone and surprise them by pulling me out of a hat. That's a sure method for wrecking an evening."

"Of course not, Steve, I wouldn't do that. What do you think I am? Don't you trust me? Come on, I'll ask, I'll set everything up. All you have to do is show up and be sociable. If you don't like her, well then you never have to go out with her again, do you? Who knows, maybe you'll hit it off nicely. In any event, she won't bite." Little did Jim know; it was a good thing that he didn't promise.

The evening started okay, with the four of us going out for pizza. My conversation was rather clumsy and stunted. As able as I had been at retaliating verbally to insults thrust at me by my former schoolmates at Wilmer Heights, I was tongue-tied when it came to having a simple conversation with girls. Jim and Robyn carried most of the conversation, but Jim did it with such natural ease that my own awkwardness was barely felt. After wolfing down several pizzas we walked over to Robyn's house. She suggested that we come over and watch a video movie. Her parents had flown to a wedding in Vancouver for the weekend and had taken her younger brother and sister with them. I was rather apprehensive, fearing that Pam wasn't too excited about the prospect of spending more time with me. But when Jim insisted, Pam actually voiced her own desire that I come along too. So I did.

We sat on the sofa in the dimly lit heated basement of Robyn's house and watched video movies. By the second movie, Jim and Robyn were already snuggled together, with Jim's arm around her shoulder. Before long, Jim and Robyn quietly crept off the couch and headed into Robyn's basement bedroom, softly shutting the door behind them. Pam looked at me, smiling hesitantly and began to snuggle closer to me. We kissed several times, and Pam flipped off the video and led me over to the bedroom of Richard, Robyn's younger brother.

Pam was a tall, pretty girl with dark, straight hair and an appealing figure. We rolled about on little Richard's narrow single bed, and I started to feel the flame that Suzy had been the first to kindle suddenly stir up. Recalling those many long and exciting hours with Suzy, I began to unbutton Pam's shirt and slide my hands over her flesh, hoping to extricate her bra. But Pam wasn't Suzy; I would soon learn that Suzy had been years ahead of her time. For good or for bad, she had got me accustomed to a certain type of sexual relationship, with its own pace. That pace, I was to discover, somewhat painfully, was not the pace at which this present relationship was fated to develop—at least according to Pam. Before I had even managed to disrobe her, I felt her teeth sink brutally into my wrist. Thinking of poor little Richard, and not wanting to bleed all over his narrow bed, I fled to the washroom and rinsed my bleeding wrist in the sink, putting pressure

155

on the wound to stop the flow of the blood. I hoped that she hadn't hit an artery.

At first I was very puzzled. I thought that this was one of those "love games" that people like to play. But very quickly, I realized that the bite was definitely an attempt to voice displeasure in my actions—namely, from progressing passionately from a little kissing to some bodily contact. By the time I got out of the washroom, with the flow of blood more or less halted, Pam had already informed Robyn and Jim that I was "some kind of pervert" and had donned her winter clothes and left. I could say little more than "I'm sorry, I think there was a misunderstanding." And then, "I'll let myself out." But Jim wouldn't desert me even after ruining his evening.

On the walk home through the cold night, I explained to Jim about my sexual relationship with Suzy, my only experience with the opposite sex. Jim laughed and gave me a long lecture, telling me how the girls at this school were very much afraid of any form of sex, because their mothers had warned them to save themselves for marriage.

"How do you manage with Robyn, then?" I asked, puzzled again.

"With patience," Jim replied. "These girls are not brave or experienced like your Suzy. You need to make them feel comfortable, to make them understand that their mothers' threats and warnings are ridiculous in this day and age. Once they feel that you no longer pose a threat, things will move along. But you've got to work at it. It takes time to develop."

"Jim?" I asked.

"What?"

"I don't think that I can ever trust you again."

"Why the hell not?"

"You promised me that Pam wouldn't bite. Now I might need a rabies shot."

"Come on, let's get you home and bandaged up properly. Grandpa Joe will go nuts when he sees this. What'll you tell him?

If you say it was a dog, he really will take you for rabies shots."

"I'll tell him it was a dog, but that mom will give me the shots. He won't dare speak to her."

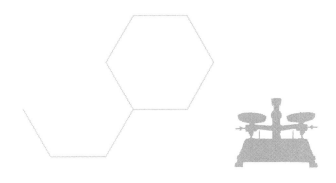

CHAPTER THIRTEEN

The day had finally arrived. Tonight I would be dining with Dr. Julia Kearns. For the first time in years, I felt that perhaps there was a chance to save myself from eternal bachelorhood—that there was someone out there who I might possibly be able to live with, someone for whom I would be willing to sacrifice my principles. I would even be prepared to sleep on the other side of the bed if necessary, if and when it came to that. I was nervous and my palms were sweaty throughout the entire day. Neal passed me in the hall and noted, "What's the matter, Steve, you look like you just saw a ghost?"

I replied flippantly, something vague about scientists not believing in ghosts, and continued along on my way, my confidence ebbing slowly. I must build myself up to prepare for this encounter. I must force myself to abandon my normally reticent behavior and be open with Julia. Who knows, I thought nervously, this could be a one-time chance. If our evening doesn't work out and Julia sees us as hopelessly incompatible, we may really end up exclusively as co-applicants on a grant. My heart burned at the thought of this. I had a sinking feeling that no matter how far I looked, I would be unlikely to find such a rare combination of understanding, confidence, and strong physical attraction.

During the morning, I was convinced several times that my watch had stopped working; I had been sneaking glances at it so often that time appeared to stand still. There was an early departmental seminar, with one of Smithers' newer students discussing a recent article on Parkinson's disease. I found myself yawning continuously, finding it difficult to concentrate on the critical discussion. Neal broke me out of my reverie by attacking the experimental basis in the article chosen. Tracy, the new student who was delivering the seminar, had obviously not thought out the significance of the experimental design chosen by the authors in a very complete context. I noticed a very interesting feature common to these "journal club" seminars. The idea was to bolster the critical abilities of the students in the department and increase their powers of assessment when examining new articles in the literature. Every week a different student was responsible for choosing a recently published article. At the seminar, the student had to present the background necessary for understanding the research achieved, discuss the experiments done, and study the conclusions that could be attained. For some reason, the students who chose a certain article (which almost inevitably was related to their own work) would defend the authors right down the line. Even more intriguingly, the lab director whose student had prepared the discussion would also almost inevitably support the work done in the article. It was almost as though he or she had done the work. I found it difficult to comprehend. Neal was pointing out legitimate criticism that perhaps did not altogether nullify the research presented in the article, but his comments certainly did cast some doubt on the relevance of some of the conclusions drawn in that particular study. Before I could snap right out of my own reverie, Smithers had turned the discussion into a free-for-all, and was lecturing Neal on the credibility of *his own research*, with no connection to the article. Neal was answering as he should, so I delayed stepping in to the argument. "Professor Smithers," he said politely, "if you have some good critical comments regarding the experiments that we're doing now, perhaps Steve and I could sit and discuss some of your ideas with you, if you have the time. But what I don't understand is how that's connected to the article that Tracy chose. There are all kinds of control experiments missing there—"

I could see that Lewis Smithers' face was turning beet red, and I wasn't particularly eager to witness a face-off between him and Neal. I cut in swiftly, "I'm sure Lewis will be able to make time to discuss some of our own experimental problems, Neal. Let's just sum up Tracy's article by saying that though the conclusions are probably correct, if that research would have come from a modest little lab like our own, we might have had trouble getting it published. It's far easier for some of those big American groups with all the political connections."

That seemed to pacify Smithers, and Neal was tactful enough to realize that there was no point in beginning a head-to-head confrontation in front of the entire department.

The day seemed to drag on interminably. I had Opera-Singh in to discuss his recent results and almost really lost my patience. He could be so stubborn sometimes that I honestly found it hard to understand how I could put up with him. Opera-Singh's main pet peeve was a forceful hatred of changing plans. This type of dislike is just not conducive to research, since every new experiment is built on the results of previous ones. There is a constant need to change and modify in order to advance. Opera-Singh didn't seem to have the adaptability necessary for this kind of work; he preferred experiments that were set up weeks in advance and balked at any last minute changes. He defined a "last minute change" as a plan modified even several days in advance. It was beyond his grasp to understand that those changes just might save his experiment and free him from the necessity of repeating it again and again because it did not work.

I finally disentangled myself from Opera-Singh and called in Neal to begin discussing the review article that we were planning. We flipped together through some sample volumes of the journal, looked up additional review papers in the online version, and decided that our article should be no more than eight to ten pages long with no more than 150 references. We set out a skeleton plan, trying to decide which aspects we would cover and which topics would remain outside the scope of our work. This was no easy matter; everything seemed important, but I've learned that it's crucial to cut right from the start. From my experience, it's almost impossible to cut a twenty page paper down to ten pages. The paper must be written from the start with the intention of being about ten pages in length; otherwise, it's virtually impossible to trim the original manuscript.

I found myself unable to eat any lunch and had to busy myself scanning the electronic journals online. I then began methodical PubMed searches. The National Institutes of Health in the United States used its Public Library of Medicine to catalog all of the significant biomedical journals; at a click researchers can use key words to identify new papers in their field or search for papers published by specific authors. Occasionally I would amuse myself electronically "spying" on colleagues and other researchers to monitor their productivity. When even that couldn't hold my attention, I wandered over to the lab to check up on my students. Neal was his usual self, hands flying and timers buzzing, with both Tania's lithe figure and Ken's cumbersome form following him around the room like shadows. They obviously understood that Neal was equipped to get them into working action and were intent on grabbing every available tip. I stood in the corner, watching but keeping my mouth closed. There was no question that from a practical standpoint, Neal could give them more than I could. I no longer had the necessary "touch" for this kind of work. I had been relegated to desk work—thinking, planning, instructing, and advising. I had lost my feeling for all the little tricks that make things work. But I was not depressed with the turn of things. Research has its dynamics and normally progresses from stage to stage. I felt that it was much better to be in charge of the research, planning the ideas and making the major decisions. The technical side was a stage that had to be overcome by every lab director; we all had had to prove our own prowess at the technical side. Now was the time for a newer generation of scientists, such as Neal, to exhibit their own mastery of the technical work, while learning to be independent by absorbing the theoretical aspects from their lab directors. Many lab directors often regretted having to do administrative paperwork and would have preferred continuing to "dirty their own hands" with their test tubes. I certainly didn't. I wasn't afraid of the hard work but could well remember the way things generally were "on the workbench." The working technical scientist first had to develop a system or methodology to support or disprove the point he had chosen. This could be fun as it necessitated theoretical research. It meant scouring the published literature to find if anyone else had already provided a fitting solution to the question asked. If not, often a custom-made solution was necessary. Once the idea had been formulated, properly thought out with the right controls and tests to see that it was feasible and in working order, the experiment could be calibrated. Once calibrated and ready for use on the particular system for which it had been designed, the excitement begins. Will it work? Will the results be as expected or a surprise? All these stages were still stages that I had enjoyed taking on. The problem for me was from that point onward. After the initial elation, there were often pitfalls. Because one was working with biological systems, after a fascinating, informative experiment, it would sometimes be difficult to repeat the results. Either the mice behaved differently, or the stock solutions had to be remade, or new reagents had to be ordered from different batches. Even the deionized water that we used in the experiments would sometimes differ in its level of deionization and pH (the degree of its acid/base composition). These and many other factors could all affect the final results. No lab director would dare publish results that hadn't been clearly repeated at least three to four times. A retraction of one's results and conclusions published in a scientific journal was about the most embarrassing thing a scientist could do. Thus, I definitely did not miss the weeks and weeks attempting to repeat an experiment that had "worked" once or twice, but for obscure technical reasons could not be repeated a third and fourth time. No, I would be more than satisfied to leave these manipulations in the capable hands of Neal and others; the preoccupation with repeating the experiments left little time for actual thinking and planning ahead. I was glad to allow Neal to repeat the experiments and obviously did my best to help bail him out when plagued by the technical problems that escaped no scientist, not even Neal.

As I watched from the side of the lab, detached from the events happening within, I could hear Neal explaining to his charges, "It's better to spin down the cells in this centrifuge. The advantage is that it has swing-out buckets and that way the cell pellet will be even and it'll be easier to remove the supernatant after the spin." I tried to recall, but couldn't remember, whether I had taught that to him or whether he had simply absorbed the information by himself.

I checked up on Opera-Singh, who never was particularly happy to see me in the lab. "I am being very busy today," he would say to me on any number of occasions. "I am not meaning to be rude, but I am not having time to discuss now," he would continue. I didn't like to make him feel pressured. It was bad enough that he had a moderately high level of "boss syndrome"; that is, he appeared to be constantly afraid of what I would say or think. On the other hand, that didn't impede his headstrong and adamant arguments with me, which occasionally bordered on the absurd.

After checking up on my mail and my e-mail and listening to my phone messages one more time, I noticed that the time had finally rounded out to almost five o'clock. That was enough for me. On the one hand, I felt that my nervousness was preventing me from accomplishing anything at work. On the other hand, I was a little bit afraid to get home too early. After taking Compo out for his daily double, what would I do for the next three hours? At least here at the lab, the time seemed to pass more quickly.

There were always intrigues, arguments, e-mail, and phone calls. At home things were far quieter. I decided to go home anyway, and then I remembered that I had wanted to clean up the apartment a little, perhaps vacuum out the carpets. Maybe Julia would come back for coffee. Perhaps she would stay longer. But then I remembered little Debby and wondered with whom Julia would entrust her care for the evening. Was Julia's ex-husband even in the city? My ex-wife wasn't, which certainly didn't bother me. But then again, I had a dog, not a six-year-old daughter.

I drove home through the slippery streets, unused to the rush-hour traffic. I usually managed to get in to the lab before peak traffic in the morning, and I would leave once the traffic had calmed down in the evening. I stopped and picked up a small cake from a nearby bakery, as well as some more fresh milk for my espresso coffee maker. Who knew how things would develop and where little Debby might spend the night. She had grandparents who lived in the city, that much I remembered.

Compo was glad to see me as usual but was slightly surprised at the hour. He must have been fast asleep on the sofa because he still seemed only half awake even as he climbed all over me and I went into my traditional defense posture. I didn't particularly feel like starting the evening off by paw-induced partial castration.

We went out for a double with Compo yellowing the snow around his favorite fire hydrant. I buried his "number one" with some more snow, and we headed back up to my flat. It always amazed me how that dog understood elevators. Sometimes I let him whiz up the three flights of stairs on his own and he would meet me coming out of the elevator. On the way down, he also knew there were two options. At the right end of the hall were the stairs. If we took the stairs at that end of the hall, he knew that we would head straight out the building door afterwards. On the other hand, if we turned left to the elevator, he knew that after getting out of the elevator on the ground floor, we would have to retrace our steps to the southwest entrance by turning back to where the stairs were. I found myself hoping that Julia would also find him amusing; she didn't even know about Compo. Then, I started to think about little Debby. How would she get along with Compo? Would Compo be jealous if new people entered my life? Some dogs became irate when their masters became parents, taking out their rage on the helpless infant who was new in the family. I blotted out these thoughts and started to get myself ready for the evening. I didn't know exactly in what way, but I had the feeling that this was going to be no ordinary evening.

Since we lived on opposite sides of the city, Julia had proposed that we meet at the restaurant, coming in separate cars. Driving through the city streets, I found myself flipping almost randomly through the Toronto radio stations, humming along and singing songs that I didn't even know. Where I managed to learn the words was a mystery to me. I suppose that the modern music lyrics, which included such diverse elements as "Love, you're the one, Love, you're my fun" were not particularly difficult to pick up, even for someone as musically challenged as me. Especially when they were repeated twenty-six times as a seemingly never-ending chorus.

Although I had done everything in my power to delay my departure from the lab and later from the apartment, I still managed to arrive more than twenty minutes early. I took my time parking the car, tidying up the array of parking tickets and gas bills that littered my dashboard. I wasn't too demanding with myself in my level of tidiness, since I knew that in any event Julia wouldn't ride in my car this evening. I finally climbed out and entered the restaurant, Las Brisas, a new Chilean restaurant that Jim swore had excellent fish, seafood, and grilled meat. Nigel claimed that this was the best place in town for a decent bottle of wine, or even a pint of "Schop," the Chilean word for draft beer. I hadn't been there myself, but Jim and Carol had given the place such a high rating that I felt it would be appropriate.

I hung up my heavy winter jacket and sat down at a comfortably pleasant two-seater table not far from the hearth-warming log fire. A glance at my watch revealed that there were still sixteen minutes left until our scheduled meeting. I decided not to order a drink until Julia arrived but to sit patiently and wait for her. I sat with my eyes transfixed on the fireplace, watching the orange-red color dance lightly and occasionally engulf the bluish tones that would sometimes surface from the log. I wondered if this symbolized a turning point in my personal life. Then the cool, cruel voice of reason pervaded my thoughts, "You're a scientist, not an expert on literary symbolism. What the hell do you know?" Before I could shake myself out of these alarming daydreams, I looked up into the pretty eyes of Julia Kearns.

"Hi, Steve. I'm glad you're early, too. I didn't relish the thought of sitting here alone and waiting for you for ten whole minutes."

"Hi, Julia. Am I glad to see you! I was about to count the tiles on the ceiling. I guess we're both early birds." She laughed easily with that delightful chuckle of hers.

While she was seating herself, I recounted the story of my own experience with chronic lateness years ago when I was a teaching assistant during my Ph.D. "Professor Rogers was in charge of this horribly boring lab course that all the undergrad biology students had to take. It was called Basic Medical Microbiology, or something like that. It was a huge course with about two hundred students and at least ten of us teaching assistants."

"I think I took a course like that in medical school," Julia nodded. "It was terrible."

"I didn't mind the teaching all that much, although it was boring doing those same basic bacteriology experiments, year after year. What drove me out of my mind were those weekly staff meetings. Old Professor Rogers would go on and on for hours trying to ensure that we lab instructors passed on the finer points of bacteriology. He used to get so wound up about how to explain the theories to the students that someone once said to me, 'He's either going to have a heart attack or an orgasm.' Unfortunately, when the old man heard the word 'orgasm,' he thought someone said 'organism' and went on for another half hour discussing the different types of bacterial organisms."

Julia laughed and threw back her pretty hair. From her re-laxed manner and easy laughter, I myself felt very comfortable and confident that the evening would be a success. She pressed me a little, "Steve, why did you remember that episode all of a sudden?"

What a mushbrain I am, I thought to myself. "Sorry, Julia, I must have mush in my brain," I said quickly, not searching for a more eloquent way of putting it. "I got to that whole story because I learned an interesting lesson about people like us—people who come on time. For every one of those gruesome staff meetings, the old professor and about half of the teaching assistants would per-petually come ten to fifteen minutes late. When the meeting was set for two o'clock, they would always show up between two and 2:15, each one with an array of excuses that varied greatly. Some showed originality, changing their reasons with every meeting, while for others, it was always the same 'I was in the middle of an experiment,' 'Got trapped in the elevator,' or 'The car wouldn't start.' Professor Rogers himself never even bothered to explain his own tardiness. He took it for granted that everyone should wait for him. After the first few months, several of us punctual types decided that there was no point coming on time; we too would come ten to fifteen minutes late. On that day, I caught my-self glancing at my watch, slowing myself as I climbed the stairs, stopping in the men's room though I didn't need to, and getting a drink of water when I wasn't even thirsty. Even after all that, I was only four minutes late and still the first one there. So there you have it; obsessive-compulsive on-time behavior."

Julia laughed again, and agreed pleasantly, "I see your point."

While we were flipping through the menu and sipping some white Chilean wine called Gato Blanco, Julia pulled a small mo-bile phone out of her purse and apologized profusely, "I really despise the overuse of these things, but Debby's got a pretty bad cold and some fever and I didn't want to call off this evening. "

"Oh, Julia, don't be silly. I must say I really appreciate your going out of your way to see me tonight. I can't even express how much I've been looking forward to this."

After ordering our meal, I began to tell Julia a little about how things were progressing in my lab. Suddenly, I felt immensely silly. Here I was, finally facing off with this woman I admired greatly and was in the process of developing affections for, and yet, I was busy telling her about my lab. The whole idea had been to get away from all that. I apologized for my inconsiderateness and tried to change the topic rapidly.

"Steve," Julia replied patiently, with that clever smile of hers, "it's alright. In fact, I think it would be rather unusual if we didn't talk some 'shop talk.' After all, your research and my psychiatric practice aren't really just jobs. We both seem to see them as more than a simple nine-to-five career. With us, I think it's more like a way of life. It's not that other things in life are not important or are even less important to us, it's just that we bend them around our work to some degree."

Listening to Julia, I felt as though I had known her for years. She had such a natural way of making me comfortable. She was so utterly agreeable, yet at the same time, so accomplished. I found it hard to see how she could hold such a fine balance. I had the feeling that if I were more agreeable, I'd be less accomplished. Not that my accomplishments would mean very much anyway if I didn't get my tenure. Stop, I kicked myself, I don't want to think of that tonight.

"You know, Julia, having had an opportunity to see some of the work you do, or at least hear a little about the situations you face every day and the people you treat, I feel frustrated with my own chosen career."

Now I could see the surprise in Julia's eyes. "You feel frustrated? Do you realize what it's like when I get a schizophrenic who doesn't respond to medication? Do you know how frustrating that is? How many lives can be ruined? How many times have I done everything but actually get down on my knees and pray that a bipolar disorder patient responds to his lithium treatment? That he actually continues to take his medication? We clinicians really feel what helplessness is."

"But at least you get to see cases where there's improvement, where your judgment and experience actually benefit some of these people. They go back and lead normal lives. Look at my side. We researchers sit in our labs, begging for money with these grant applications, writing these bombastic statements at the end of each application saying how this research 'may ultimately lead to the development of new therapeutics blah blah blah.' Do I really believe that? How many grants have I written that ever helped turn out some new drug? Will I ever discover anything that might even help in the design of a drug, something that might actually make a difference?"

"Steve, don't be so hard on yourself. You know how scientific research is built up like bricks in a wall. How many grants have you actually written? How long has it been since you wrote your very first grant? You can't objectively judge right now whether your research is leading somewhere. Perhaps it may not, but neither you nor anyone else in the scientific community can foresee that right now. I feel that you are lucky—you always have that eternal hope ahead of you. We clinicians are stuck with our experience and limited repertoire of drugs. If one doesn't work, we try another. If that is also no good, we combine or up the dose. It's almost like alchemy. At least you have a logical basis behind your actions. Our clinical logic is masked by the experience factor. When we give seretonin reuptake absorbers, like Prozac, to depressed people, we don't sit and wonder about the biochemical pathways involved. We wonder about the dose, the combination with other drugs, and the possible complications. I think it would be refreshing to actually spend time learning about how these drugs work."

"I don't know, Julia, sometimes I feel very hopeless. All this tedious work and how far has it got us?"

Julia looked at me wisely, a hint of a smile curled at the corner of her lips. "Oh I think that once you get your tenure, your confidence in your work will spring back. I'm not worried about that."

"Maybe we should switch jobs for a while and see how it goes," I said jokingly.

Julia's eyes lit up, "I'd like that Steve, I really would. But I wouldn't know a molecule from an atom or a mole from a hedgehog."

"You'd make a great researcher, Julia," I encouraged, "but you'd have to deal with Smithers and his gang and all the politics in my department. It's a rat race, publishing articles, grants, teaching, and all the strife between the people in the department. Sometimes I wonder how I don't end up hospitalized in your department. But something puzzles me, Julia. I always thought, and no hard feelings with the generalization, that you doctors were always so proud and full of what you do that most of you wouldn't trade your profession for any other."

"In general, that's true, but I think it's just a pose. The grass is always greener on the neighbor's lawn. The only difference is that doctors hold a certain power—the power to heal and the power not to heal. That can be a heavy responsibility to bear. For some, it's equivalent to the power of being a commander in the army or the manager of a company. Those are the doctors to look out for and stay away from."

"I know exactly what you mean," I said sipping my wine enjoyably. I felt almost as though someone were echoing my thoughts. Maybe she did read minds. I related to her the tremendous feelings of inferiority that doctors sometimes induced in researchers. Julia was quite taken aback.

"You researchers feel inferior? Why, because you can't prescribe drugs? You can buy them at the lab for your research! Seriously, doctors may feel themselves superior, but I'm amazed that researchers play their game and stoop to feeling inferior. I wouldn't have imagined it."

"Julia, I was at a conference in Boston recently, and one of the bigwigs, Bob Simonsen—you must have heard of him?" Julia nodded, her eyes twinkling elegantly. "Well, he wanted to stress how important it is that more money be allocated to basic research. He was emphasizing that doctors, good as they may be, are limited by a lack of good drugs. His point was that the development of those drugs will only come from long-term investments in basic research, in understanding why things are as they are. It was a real plug for more money for us basic researchers. At any rate, to stress the perceived differences in status between doctors and researchers, he flashed two cute slides during the lecture: In the first one, a headwaiter is about to seat a group of gentlemen at a table in a restaurant. He says, 'Dr. Smith—are you a medical doctor or *just* a Ph.D.?' In the second slide, another waiter is seating another group of scientists, and the waiter asks politely, 'What occupation do you gentlemen have?' One of them answers, 'We're cell biologists.' The waiter looks puzzled, and then finally asks, 'I'm sorry, what is it that you sell?' So you see how physicians and the general public don't exactly think too highly of basic researchers."

Julia laughed at the anecdotes. I could tell that she was amused, but I knew that she was hoping I didn't categorize her with the rest of her medical profession.

"Maybe I should have been a psychologist, then," said Julia. "That does sound a little tricky, being in your situation."

"I think I would have chosen social work. Psychologists are for the elite—those who can afford it. But if my grandfather heard me say that right now, he'd be very angry."

Julia looked at me with surprise, for the second time that evening, "You have a grandfather who's still alive? How old is he? Where does he live? And why would he be angry with you if you had become a social worker?"

Suddenly I felt as though I were under hypnosis, like the time when a psychologist had helped me try to get over my separation from Jeannie several years ago. The entire restaurant was blocked out; all I focused on was Julia's calm face, her greenish eyes. I told her about Grandpa Joe caring for dad during my childhood. She hadn't forgotten that I mentioned having a father who was stricken by bipolar disorder. I explained Grandpa Joe's hatred of anything that reminded him, even remotely, of communist Russia: labor parties, social workers, anything in the

172

color red. I related how I had left my Regina home immediately after high school, arriving in Toronto both to seek higher education and to get away from the turmoil at home. I recounted how psychiatric disorders and their roots and causes had become an obsession with me. Perhaps they had become my own form of absolution, repentance, my personal "Hail Marys" for abandoning my father. I explained about mom and Paul, and how they had moved here to Toronto about ten years later, finally freed of their financial obligations in Regina. They still looked out for Ervin and Cindy. Julia was especially interested in hearing about Delia, Paul's daughter. She was in and out of alcoholic dry-out centers every few years, and mom and Paul spent a tremendous amount of time worrying about her and trying to cope with her problems. I answered Julia's many questions, telling her that Grandpa Joe was now over eighty-five years of age, and still one hundred percent "with it," caring for dad in the same house on Wascana Drive. Cindy's husband, Wayne, had recently taken over Grandpa Joe's business officially, but Grandpa Joe was still running dad's life, with his characteristic optimism, trying to get him out working and even remarried.

These memories evoked very strong feelings; I couldn't remember ever opening myself up to someone like this. After all, Julia was, until now, really only a work collaborator. I could feel myself falling for Julia, for her charm, her wisdom, and her clarity.

"You know Julia, I don't think I've ever been able to tell anyone all that much about my private family life—and it's not the Gato Blanco. I hope you don't feel like some sort of psychologist right now."

"But Steve," she chided me gently, "we both just finished professing our desire to be counselors or social workers. Seriously, though, I'm really glad you saw me worthy to confide in. You have an amazing history, a very special family. I really understand what brought you to choose your chosen career. And I'm convinced that you have chosen the right one."

"Julia, before I say anything stupid or ruin the evening, I'd like to ask you to go out with me again. I really feel, well, happy here with you. I realize that you've got to get home to Debby tonight, otherwise I'd love to go on talking with you all night. That's the only reason I don't invite you over for coffee right now."

"It's true, I've got to get back and let the sitter go, but please come back and have coffee with me. I've got a little espresso machine. I even baked a pie."

There were tears of happiness in my eyes as I took her hand and we walked to the parking lot to our respective cars.

CHAPTER FOURTEEN

I drove carefully through the dark, icy streets, filled with a feeling of personal joy that had been sorely lacking in me for many years. It definitely was not the type of self-centered egoistic lust that had induced me to seek gratification in Duffy's enticing embrace. That whole episode seemed to have occurred months earlier, even years ago. I was having trouble recalling the pretty features of Duffy's face. In all fairness, though, we were only really face-to-face for a short time in the Mexican restaurant. At the hockey game we had faced the ice below us, and in her flat we had made love in the dark. All I really remembered clearly was her funny little hat and the earring pierced through her nostril.

My mind put Duffy on a dusty shelf and returned to thoughts of Julia. I searched my own previous experiences for some basis of comparison and for some way of understanding my own newly developed feelings. Although it was definitely not one of those encounters based entirely on sexual feelings, it was also clearly not asexual, platonic, or neutered. No, it's true that the presence of little Debby, who had been ill during the night with terrible fits of coughing, had perhaps set the tone and pace for our night together. But that didn't matter. Not at all. In truth, I felt very secure. Watching Julia swiftly rise from the warm bed, dress hastily and quickly pacify Debby provided me with a very pleasant form of relief. She fed her half an aspirin, set up a humidifier in her room, read to her, and waited until she fell back asleep, breathing regularly, if somewhat heavily. I struggled to define my own feelings, an endeavor at which I considered myself on a scale from one to ten to be somewhere in the negative range. I estimated that Jeannie would also have rated me with a similar score.

As hard as I tried to fight it, to stay in control, I felt strong flashes of elation and achievement. It felt as though an earthquake had shaken my very foundations and had uprooted my life-long priorities. Suddenly, I didn't care about my tenure. All at once, I began to lose interest in my research, my grants, publications, curriculum vitae, and the rest of those formerly precious matters. In a single spark, there was a general floundering of my concern for mom and Paul, for the delicate situation back in Regina, and for world news in general. I thought to myself, the hell with Smithers, the hell with pompous old Professor Stillby, the hell with my course and teaching. These things seemed not to matter anymore. I found myself noticing something that had previously escaped my thoughts. Perhaps this was because I had never been in a situation remotely similar to this one before. To my astonishment, I realized that I showed all the classical symptoms of depression, the behavior of someone in mourning. I realized that many of these symptoms seemed to overlap with what I suspected were feelings of love. How could this be? Was this plausible? That love and depression could stir a similar array of feelings or, as we scientists might contend, stimulate similar or parallel biochemical pathways? I asked myself excitedly, is depression a state of unfulfilled love, of aborted love, or love that has gone off the proper path? Are depressed people blessed with an aptitude for love that escapes ordinary mortals, skeptics in the realm of romantic love? Love. Now there's a word whose usage I had been cautiously avoiding for my entire life. What does it mean? Look it up in the dictionary and you come out more confused than before you even started. With Jeannie, I hadn't believed in love. Neither of us had ever expressed our "love" for one another. That's not really a fair example, because the communications were so bad between us that it was like comparing snail mail with e-mail. We never expressed *any* feelings, never mind love. I remember once propounding my theory of mating between the sexes to Jeannie, angrily rejecting the term "love" as being "a pot of clichés sewn together like a fishing net." I had insisted that relationships developed out of a random-like convenience; a man meets a woman, and they interact—live together, have sex together, and take care of each other. If this is beneficial to both sides, more or less in an equal fashion, the relationship succeeds and proceeds onward. If not, there is a break, and each person commences searching again until he or she meets another potential partner. Sometimes that comes quickly; sometimes it takes years. It depends on the standards set by each individual and the number of potentially available, unattached people that we meet. I called this my stochastic theory for human mating. I borrowed it, of course, from the scientific world. At that time, only science had any meaning for me. In chemistry, we scientists maintain that the molecules everywhere, in every material, including air, constantly move in a random-like motion, known as Brownian motion. Heating up the air, then, would be equivalent to socializing. In both cases, these events would increase the statistical chance of a meeting or interaction between two molecules or, in my analogy, between two people. My feelings for Julia were beginning to cast doubts on these radically interesting but somewhat oversimplistic theories of human behavior. Although "chance" meetings certainly determined with whom I would interact and perhaps eventually form a relationship, my feelings of elation from being with Julia were beginning to teach me that within my so-called stochastic system, there were various degrees of successful mating—levels that I had obviously not attained in previous relationships. Perhaps love wasn't such a difficult word to use: I simply hadn't tasted its real meaning; I had only seen glimpses of what it was supposed to mean. And like my attitude toward many nonscientific subjects, I had been especially skeptical.

I parked my car in the lot under my building and took the elevator up. It was still dark outside, and I hadn't slept for even a moment all night. There had been too much to talk about. I hadn't been able to feel entirely free with Julia until I had poured my entire brief, but recent episode with Duffy off my chest. She had squeezed me gently and said, "I don't want to be with a celibate." Thinking about it afterwards, I realized that a woman of Julia's stature would not be taken aback by my fling with Duffy. However, those feelings of guilt had been hitting me in the pit of my stomach now for days, ever since Julia had agreed to have dinner with me. She then quietly analyzed the situation, "Steve, do you think that you had some feelings for me even back then, when you went out with Duffy?"

I answered truthfully, "I'm certain that I did. It's just that as a scientist, one who deals in logic and reason, I found it hard to understand exactly what feelings I could have for you. After all, we never had any connection except for the start of this collaborative grant. I couldn't face the 'love at first sight' theory. It went against everything I believed in."

"I won't try to be simplistic," replied Julia, "but it's certainly not love at first sight. Talking to each other, even though the subject may have been entirely scientific, there's still more than enough of a chance to evaluate and understand one's emotions. It's not a hit-and-run thing. I've seen you in the lab, and you've seen me in the clinic. We've already both noted that our respective occupations are not just day-to-day jobs but an extension of our lives. An integral part of each of our lives. So we each examined an important part of each other's lives. That's *not* love at first sight. That's more like a careful decision based on our knowing each other quite well."

I had come home basically to take Compo out. The poor dog was always the butt of my sexual/romantic encounters, suffering with a full bladder. I had taken him out just before setting out for the restaurant the previous night, but that was still quite a few hours ago. Obviously, I had fed him well, with a few special treats to prepare him for a potentially long and lonely evening. I felt badly, but knew that there was nothing I could do. I couldn't even send him to Jeannie anymore. She was gone from both our lives. I don't know how much Compo cared or remembered her in his furry memory when she wasn't around for weeks and months. I certainly remembered her but was perfectly satisfied to relinquish her to Martin and her own new life.

When we came back up to the apartment, it was only six a.m. and far too early to prepare for work. I wandered aimlessly around the apartment, trying to get my thoughts together. Suddenly, I noticed that there were two messages on my answering machine. The first one was from Cindy, long distance from what Smithers undoubtedly considered the "hick town" of Regina. She didn't say much but left a message asking me to call, saying that she thought something might be wrong at home. Even after all those years, more than twenty years since I had left the Wascana Drive house in Regina, Cindy still called it "home." Grandpa Joe and dad were still there. Cindy had mumbled into the machine that Grandpa Joe had canceled a business meeting with her husband Wayne at the factory, something he had never done before. I couldn't help feeling that Cindy was overdoing it a little. After all, Grandpa Joe was almost eighty-six years old. Maybe he had the flu or didn't feel like going out into the freezing Regina winter that day. On the other hand, I knew Grandpa Joe. He wasn't planning on relinquishing *his say* in the company. Although he let Wayne run things, Grandpa Joe was still pulling the strings, ensuring that all the right decisions were being made. The other message was from mom. Judging from the time of the call the previous evening, I gathered that Cindy had tried my place first, but not having caught me at home, she was sufficiently worried to call mom. More than likely, she had tried to contact Paul; he was far easier to talk to, especially concerning anything to do with Grandpa Joe. Mom was less reassuring. I could imagine her telling Cindy, "Listen Cindy, Grandpa Joe may be losing it; he's been on the edge for years. There's not much you can do about it." Mom had called to ask me to return Cindy's call. Obviously, she had not had a reassuring effect on Cindy.

I looked at my watch and decided that it wasn't a good idea to call Cindy that early. She and Wayne were not early risers, and I would probably just frighten them instead of helping with anything. I had some apple juice to drink and turned on my computer to see if I had received any e-mail. I then began to yawn and lay down with the intention of taking a catnap for an hour before getting up for a busy day at work.

My "catnap" was interrupted, about four hours later, ironically, by a dog. Compo was barking frantically at the postman, who had apparently come to Mrs. Baxter next door to deliver a registered letter. I quieted Compo, explaining that there was no need to become alarmed, it was only the mail delivery. I glanced at my watch and then panicked myself. It was already nearly 10:30. I knew that by the time I got showered and shaved and crossed the morning traffic to the institute, it would be near noon. I cursed. That didn't seem to help much, so I cursed more loudly. All that did was to serve to frighten Compo, and he simply got up and left the room. He obviously felt that the dynamics of my evolving bad mood were heading downhill, and apparently he wanted no part of that. I didn't blame him, but there was some hypocrisy here, even for a dog. It was all right for him to bark at the mailman, but for me to swear at the walls was improper, at least from his standpoint. I became more practical, convinced Compo to come out with me for another daily double, and started to hurry to get myself organized and off to work. I thought rather stupidly, it's not as if I have any specific commitment this morning. Neal and Singh will handle any problems in the lab. Neal claims that I only interfere when I arrive at the scene anyway. The grant was still in Julia's hands. I had no teaching obligations today—only some results to discuss with my fellow workers and a promise to Neal to get organized with our review article. Still, I was not pleased; in fact, as Nigel would say, I was "seriously displeased." I believed in putting in a full day's work and not allowing my personal life to interfere with my professional activities. And here I was allowing my very first date with Julia to mess up an entire morning at work. I tried hard to convince myself of the insignificance of this and to look at it as a single isolated and very unique case. Still, I found it difficult to dissociate myself from the feeling that I was falling into a pattern of laziness. I left the apartment hurriedly, feeling uncomfortable. In my haste, Cindy's and mom's phone calls completely escaped my memory. After all, I could have comfortably returned their calls at 10:30 in the morning.

In the car on the way to the institute, an odd thought struck me: Why hadn't anyone from the lab called to see why I hadn't come in to work? I knew that they got along fine without me, but I had always informed them when I was going away or when I wasn't coming in to work. They knew that I lived alone. What if something had happened to me during the night? I sat wedged in midday traffic at a red light, trying to calculate how long it would take until someone discovered my body if I died suddenly in the night. Would someone from the lab finally call? Would anyone become suspicious and visit my apartment? If I didn't show up at mom and Paul's on a Friday evening, would they come look for me or would my body rot and decompose until Mrs. Baxter could smell it? Would Compo starve? The thought of that particularly frightened me. I couldn't ever remember a day where Neal didn't show up at work, except when he took his rare but usually lengthy trekking vacations. However, when Opera-Singh was ill, I had certainly called to make sure he was okay. I had called him every morning to see how he was recovering until he came back to work. I began to feel a little depressed that no one had bothered to call. At one point, quite close to the institute, I almost turned the car around and headed back home. Who needed me anyway? My elation from the previous night had faded quickly in the reality of the day.

I circled the institute complex four times before finally managing to wedge my car into a little parking spot, working up a decent sweat struggling with the rack-and-pinion steering of my little car. As usual, both elevators were on coffee break, and I hiked up the six flights breathlessly, feeling guilty for my tardiness, but nevertheless realizing that no one would even notice. Even if they did, who cared?

I unlocked my office door, peeking down the corridor expecting to see the streams of light from the two lab rooms casting bright shadows into the dimly lit hallway. To my surprise, I didn't see any shadows. In fact, from my angle it appeared as though the lab doors were actually closed. I peeked at my watch; it was already almost noon. It was impossible that there was no one in the lab at that hour. I racked my brain frantically, trying to remember if there had been any scheduled departmental seminar, but I could see that there was activity in most of the other labs. Smithers' students were pounding the hallways, marching back and forth with their usual shouts and boisterous behavior. Nussensweig was in the hall talking to Smithers, and representatives from the other departmental labs seemed to be working as usual.

I hung up my winter coat, put my personal belongings away in my office, and then sauntered down the hall in an odd state of mind. Just hours ago I had been elated; I had felt that nothing here at the institute was worth caring about. Then, a few hours later I arrive at work to find that no one was in the lab, and I could feel my heart pounding. I realized that I still cared what was happening in the lab; I simply didn't understand what could possibly be going on. They couldn't all have gone down to the main library in the middle of the day; that would be too much of a coincidence.

I moved down the corridor slowly, suspiciously, towards the two labs. My heart was pounding and a sickening feeling of nausea was overtaking my senses. While with Julia, my encounter with Duffy had seemed years ago. Now, in the corridor, approaching my lab rooms, last night with Julia also felt ages ago.

182

I finally reached the first lab and could see that the door was closed, but there was a small neon light, probably the one above Neal's desk, that was giving off an aura of odd shadows reflected on the inset glass frame of the door. I still didn't understand what was going on. An idea occurred to me. Perhaps Neal had locked the doors and closed the lights so that he could write the review without any interruptions from outside. My confidence returned slowly, and I began to turn the knob and open the door.

"Congratulations!" came out the loud cry. The lights flashed on quickly, and I felt palpitations in my heart and a lump of anxiety stuck in my throat, feeling like a poorly digested onion. I looked around me, and everyone stared at me. I must have been pale and shocked, because I remember Julia taking my hand, seating me, and pouring me a glass of cola. The entire lab was there: Neal, Opera-Singh, Tania, Ken, and even Hugo, the new-born Christian in charge of the departmental orders. Most importantly, Julia was also there.

For the second time, I glanced around the lab, surveying the surroundings. There were balloons and streamers hanging from all the shelves. The place looked more like a *Romper Room* studio than a research lab. There was a table all set with a white linen tablecloth, which contained wine and cheese and cold cuts and salads of every available type. I still didn't understand what the hell was going on. I understood that we were celebrating something. Perhaps someone's birthday? But my memory for dates was poor and there wasn't a chance that I would remember whose birthday we were celebrating. Another thought occurred to me: perhaps Neal was getting married? He had been going out for several years with a psychology student, but it didn't seem like Neal to make an issue of his own personal life. It was more fitting for him to come to work one morning and announce that he had gotten married the week before.

Neal was the perceptive one this time, even beating Julia to the quick comprehension of the situation. He turned to her and said, "He doesn't get it, does he?"

She looked at me, with that enticing smile on her lips, and turned back to Neal, "No, Neal, I don't believe he does get it. Perhaps they didn't manage to get through to him."

I was regaining my composure and started to become irate with these little mind games. I stood up, did a small but elegant pirouette around the room, looked at everyone, and calmly said, "Would someone mind telling me what the hell is going on, whose birthday or wedding we're celebrating, and why you people aren't busy at work." I added that last comment to prove that I hadn't lost control, that I was still the boss, despite my memory lapses or my inability to remember birthday parties. My message was supposed to be that whatever the case, the work must go on.

All eyes focused on Neal for the explanation. He was the natural leader. "Let's do it this way," he said, removing a white towel from an elegantly crafted cake on the table. It was shaped like the human brain. I could see the segmentation, the cerebellum poking out from below, the large chocolate-covered mass of the cerebral cortex, and the stem of the medulla leading up from what I assumed was the spinal cord to the hippocampus. Iced onto the delicious looking double-layered chocolate cheesecake, where the corpus callosum or perhaps the caudate nucleus should have been were the words: CONGRATULATIONS ON YOUR TENURE! THE LAB. I looked around me, shocked and unable to absorb the sudden turn of events. Julia must have felt the need to seat me again, afraid that I would sway and fall over on my face. I must have been sweating profusely, because I can remember wiping my forehead with a tissue. My first reaction was one of denial, "Aren't you being a little premature? I mean officially I'm still waiting for my tenure, nice though the party is."

Neal replied excitedly, "Steve, go listen to your answering machine in your office. The dean's office claimed that the secretary left at least five messages on your machine. This is for real. They tried to call you all morning at home, too, but claimed that the line was busy. They asked me to try to reach you at home. I've been trying to ring every fifteen minutes. Your phone must be out of order!"

Suddenly I recalled disconnecting the phone before my "brief catnap" and forgetting to reconnect it afterwards. I began to understand that this was for real: It was not a dream and it wasn't another of Neal's games. It was true. I had finally received my permanent position here in the institute. And even Julia was here to share these important moments with me.

"Thanks, guys," I said, beginning to fully appreciate how happy my fellow workers were for me, and how much they had done to make me feel happy too. "You name the restaurant, and you are all invited out tonight, along with the partner of your choice, to celebrate with me. Julia, I'd be delighted if you'll join us as my partner. Please bring Debby, too if she's feeling well enough."

There it was. Years of struggling and fighting for this position, striving to make it a permanent appointment, and finally it had arrived. I was supposed to be happy. Yet I was and I wasn't at the same time. The same earlier dichotomy of love/depression hounded me. I was pleased with my tenure, yes, but there was now a letdown in the adrenaline, as though I could remove my rear guard, relax, and take it easy. I wasn't sure if that was what I really wanted. Perhaps I lived for those tensions, for the adrenaline that the continuous suspense pumped into my veins. Was this dichotomy—happiness mixed with an inkling of aimlessness, tiredness, or perhaps even depression—what it was like to suffer from bipolar disorder? I reasoned that it was very different indeed, but the feeling persisted. I caught myself wondering why I was casting my father's illness on myself, something which was characteristic of people in mourning. The wives and/or husbands of heart attack victims were known to complain of psychosomatic chest pains in the first few months of mourning. This was considered a natural occurrence in the healing process of mourning. But what was I mourning? Who was I mourning? I now had my career sewn together, secure, with promise of improving and less pressure as the years rolled on. I could now spend a little more time taking care of myself and perhaps move to a better apartment. And what about Julia? There was a new, sweet, and meaningful relationship in my life—the first real promise in many years. Even mom would be pleased. I pushed away the more morbid thoughts and sent Neal to round up some of the other researchers in the department to come and have some cake. They swooped in like eagles; tasty food was always in short supply in our institute. Even Smithers himself paid tribute by coming over for a slice of cake. I watched him fork down a piece of the tasty cake after he had carefully chosen the cerebral cortex area. I recalled, *"matter over mind,"* the advice he had blessed me with years ago. I felt a surge of confidence, watching Smithers literally and unknowingly swallow his own words in a symbolic fashion. I wondered whether he remembered *that* advice that he had given me all those years ago. But then I knew: Smithers never forgot anything. If he were ever to become ill with Alzheimer's disease, he would still probably remember more than most people, even more than most scientists.

As the celebration ensued, I still felt my mixed bag of feelings. The Dean called to pass on his congratulations and explained that the reason the tenure had taken so long was purely technical. "There's no one who can fill your position in the entire institute," he assured me. "In fact, we could use a few more researchers just like you, even in the same field. It's the research of the future that you're dealing with."

I thanked him profusely and invited him over for cake and coffee, but he politely claimed that he was busy with appointments all morning. He swore that he would visit our lab within the next few weeks to discuss how we felt in the institute and what could be improved. I envisioned Neal preparing a small but essential twenty page list, perhaps beginning with the serviceability of the elevators.

The phone rang again in the lab, and Neal, with an unusual amiability, answered pleasantly. I saw him frown slightly, and he quickly trotted over to me with his cordless phone. "Steve, it's long distance from Regina," he whispered and led me to the other, empty lab and sat me down at Opera-Singh's desk. "I'll keep them out so no one will bother you."

I held the phone to my ear; it was Cindy, as I had already guessed. "Steve, I tried to get hold of you," she said and burst into tears on the phone.

"I know, Cindy. I wanted to call you back earlier, but I was afraid you'd be asleep."

"Asleep?!" she retorted, the anger temporarily halting her tears. "Who could possibly sleep? Something terrible has happened." She burst into such a strenuous round of bawling that I was forced to hold the phone away from my ear and just wait until she composed herself enough to tell what had happened.

She finally managed to compose herself enough to breathe out the words, "Grandpa Joe."

I knew that something had happened to Grandpa Joe. He was eighty-six years old, and though he had been in excellent health, there's no guaranteed security for a man of that age. I tried to comfort her, although I loved the man myself, as a grandfather, a "mother," a shaper of my own destiny.

"Cindy," I consoled, "it'll be all right. I'll get on the next plane. I understand what you and Wayne must be going through—"

She cut me off angrily, screaming through her tears, "Stop, Steve, you don't understand anything. Nothing! It's a nightmare!"

And although all the signs were there, perhaps for years, our family was particularly notorious for a poor understanding of psychology, of human nature. It's true that I didn't understand anything. The truth was far worse than anything I could ever have imagined. It was Julia who finally entered the lab and found me, perhaps an hour later, sprawled out with my face resting on my forearm, on Opera-Singh's desk, sobbing incessantly, like I never had before.

EPILOGUE

Through the partly closed blinds of my office door window I could see Neal lurking outside. "Come in, Neal," I called out and waited as he plunged into the crowded room and sank easily into a chair opposite me.

"It looks as if your botanical gardens are really blooming. Don't you feel that they're secretly competing with you for air— that they'll use it all up and suffocate you one day?"

"I didn't know that you fell for those old wives' tales, or have you developed a touch of paranoia, a drop of agoraphobia? That's why the window is open," I said, smiling up at him sarcastically.

He looked up at the open window, with a warm April breeze wafting in and observed, "It's not old wives' tales. It's all in the *Farmer's Almanac*. But when did you get the screen for your window anyway?"

"I just had it put in yesterday. I ordered it last summer, but you know how things are here in the institute."

"Do I ever!" Neal complied, and then looked puzzled. "Is your newly acquired cynicism something that's arrived with the tenure, or have I started to finally rub off on you?"

"I think it's the tenure, Neal, but I was a cynic just like you when I was doing my Ph.D. I've just matured since then."

"Or reached senescence," Neal parried.

"Point taken," I agreed. I was too tired and mentally ill-equipped to get into a debate with him. "What can I do for you this morning, Neal?"

"Nothing," he said, with a hint of a smile on his lips, "except look at this." He pulled out a new volume of the journal *Annual Review of Depressive Disorders* and plopped it onto my desk. "How do you like them apples? Fresh off the press!"

There it was—our review, published, finally in print. I flipped through the pages, examining the title. I enjoyed looking at the type, counting the number of pages, scanning the references and acknowledgments, and even examining the format in which our own names appeared, in bold, Gothic style letters. There was an immense sense of accomplishment. Neal and I had literally played "ping-pong" with that review for weeks on end after he had written the original draft. I would change the wording, reshape paragraphs, and shuffle the paragraphs to different locations. After three or four weeks of this intense "rebound" writing, Neal began to save the earlier versions that had been written prior to my corrections. He claimed that I had gotten to the point of perfection where I was actually reverting to the original draft after spending weeks making numerous changes. He was right in several instances. But here was the final product, our stamp placed firmly in this new little niche in this "field of the future," as the Dean had called it just six months ago. And what a lot had occurred since then.

I looked at Neal thoughtfully, sprawled in the chair across from me. I realized that he was doing his very best to cheer me up and get me back to my old self. Neal was Neal, with his brashness and cynical nature. Anyone who knew him as well as I did would certainly have been able to detect the subtle but definite changes in the way he had been acting towards me over the past few months. Even the way he had argued during the writing of the review had been different, more low-key and relaxed. I appreciated that very much and told him so on at least one occasion, but he always cut me off in the middle and changed the subject. Apart from my close family, comprised of mom and Paul, Cindy, Wayne, Ervin, and now Julia and little Debby, I think Neal was the one most caught up in the horrid sequence of events that commenced on the day I had received my tenure. He was more helpful and more involved than either Nigel or Jim and Carol. That may be because I had first heard the sickening news in the lab. Neal had even answered the phone on that fateful call from Cindy in Regina. But I suspected that Neal's true motivation was a desire to really help me, if possible, in his own way.

I thanked Neal for showing me our review and went back into those little reveries that had been haunting me over the past few months.

Julia herself had been a tower of strength for me. I wouldn't allow her to accompany me to the funeral along with mom and Paul, who had flown out to Regina with me on the same flight. I felt that this was something that I had to face without her, that there was no point dragging her into the midst of the horrid episode. And it had really been horrid. I had read Grandpa Joe's final letter, over and over, struggling to comprehend his motives. And I thought that I did understand. But his written words wrote me off as a failure, someone who could not be trusted. Grandpa Joe did not trust anyone in the family with the awesome burden of caring for dad, not even me. I was sure that he had not forgiven me for leaving Regina for Toronto twenty years ago, much in the same manner that he had never forgiven mom for leaving dad. I felt sickened at the thought. I now had a better understanding of how Grandpa Joe must have felt many years earlier when mom had announced her decision to leave us in the care of Ms. Telia Mastpole when my parents went away on their winter holiday. What did he mean by writing that he "didn't want to burden me with taking care of dad?" I didn't know whether I was more shocked at the realization that Grandpa Joe didn't really believe dad would ever be well enough to take care of himself or more hurt by the insulting insinuation that no one else in the family, including me, was equal to the task of taking care of him. Over the years, Grandpa Joe had always voiced such intense optimism, clarity, and confidence. It was more than just a little unnerving to think that all that time, deep within, he may have always known that there was no hope—that dad always would be in constant need of psychiatric attention either by a full-time father/son or at a psychiatric institution.

I would never know now what Grandpa Joe really felt; whether he simply didn't trust me with dad's care or whether he honestly didn't want to place any extra burden on me. Probably both theories were correct. It was more a question of which factor played a greater role in his decision. But there was no one left to ask. Grandpa Joe was now a mental vegetable, totally speechless and practically catatonic, maintained at present in a private Regina institution since the incident. He had decided that the end of his own life was near or at least that his own strength would soon ebb, leaving dad alone and without him. And Grandpa Joe had not been impressed with the limited possibilities available for taking care of dad, me among them. Through connections with my former high school "buddy," Micky Morooney, whose interests hadn't changed much over the past twenty years, Grandpa Joe had managed to purchase a small handgun. Some things never changed. More accurately, some people never changed. Grandpa Joe's classical plan, as outlined in the letter still sitting locked in my desk drawer, had been to "put father out of his misery" and then take his own life. Unfortunately, at least for Grandpa Joe, the gun had jammed after he had shot and killed dad by putting a single neat hole through his brain while he was asleep. When the police arrived after being called by worried neighbors, according to their version, they had found Grandpa Joe sobbing softly, one hand around dad's rapidly cooling body, the other still clutching the jammed little handgun. Those were the last sounds that Grandpa Joe ever uttered. For all practical purposes, he had committed suicide. By the time mom, Paul, and I had arrived in Regina, Cindy and Wayne had informed us that there was absolutely nothing anyone could do for Grandpa Joe. He responded to nothing. He wouldn't eat or drink and had to be fed intravenously. He had wanted to die and be together with his only son. Even if that wish had failed physically, both mentally and emotionally Grandpa Joe had achieved his goal.

The phone rang and I picked it up. Due to my edginess, I would often wait to see who was calling on the machine and only then pick up the phone. This time I forgot, but I was lucky.

"Hi, Steve. How are you doing?"

"Fine, Julia, and you?"

"Not too badly. I've got some more blood samples for you. Things are progressing just like you wrote in the grant."

"Yes, we might even get additional funds for follow-up studies next year. By the way, Julia, if you finish early enough this afternoon, maybe we'll stop and buy groceries at the supermarket on the way home."

"Sure, Steve, good idea. We're running low in several things. Listen, I called because I just received another FAX from the Regina Whitehorn Psychiatric Institute. They've finally agreed to transfer him to Toronto at the end of the month and relinquish him to the care at the Intercity Institute here. I know that means a lot to you; I do rounds at the Intercity, and I suppose that you may finally feel as though the circle is closing."

"Yes, thanks, Julia. I don't know what I would have done without you. I don't know what I would do without you. Yes, I think that I'll finally feel as though I'm doing something, as though I'm still capable of proving to Grandpa Joe that I could have taken the responsibility, if not for dad, at least for Grandpa Joe. Or what used to be the real Grandpa Joe. I suppose that you're right, the circle is closing. But sometimes I have an unreasonable feeling that the radius is still the same length. I hope that will change with time."

I said good-bye, put down the receiver, closed the shades of my door, and locked it from the inside. I sat and cried and cried and cried, trying to turn the circle inside out, until I could no longer feel the difference between depression and elation.

ACKNOWLEDGMENTS

I would like to thank my own family, Naava, Mika and Eylon — *for being my family*. What would I do without you?! I'd also like to thank Aubrey and Phil Caplan for bearing with me throughout this long journey. Many thanks to Kathy Bubbeo for a superb job editing, and Kim Goldberg for bringing the cover to life. I would also like to thank Dr. John Inglis for his kind advice and encouragement.

Made in the USA
Charleston, SC
21 October 2010